the **SLOW**KILL

Nancy Smith

This book is a work of fiction. Names, characters, places and incidents are either a product of the author's imagination or used fictitiously. Any similarity to actual persons, living or dead, or events is entirely coincidental.

The Slow Kill

Author: Nancy Smith
Printed in the United States
Published 2014
Republished 2023
First Look Publishing (Austin)
www.nancysmithwriter.com
Version 1.8
ISBN Number 978-0-9913907-0-0
Cover Design: Brian Burrowes
Editor: Wendy Wheeler
Editor: Kirkus Edits
Editor: Yellowbird Editors

This book is dedicated to
Polly Enders, who has read everything I've ever written.

CONTENTS

ACKNOWLEDGMENTS

Many thanks to Eduardo Garcia, Mike Keenan, Andrea Hendricks, and David Barnett for their valued input and support.

Part I

Chapter 1

June 2035

Hot. Scorching hot.

The weather forecaster blamed another unmoving high-pressure system for creating the relentless heat that daily shrouded them in triple-digit temperatures.

Frank Harvey ran. He hated jogging, but it settled his mind and loosened his muscles. He found his pace. His old cross-trainers, held together by layers of duct tape, slapped the path as Old Sol beat down on his shoulders. The sun had barely peeked over the horizon and he was sweating, but not as much as he would have thought. There was no moisture in the air. There was no moisture in him.

Frank zigzagged a dirty path lined with the dried and broken limbs of hackberry trees. The leaves left on the trees had turned brown before reaching maturity making it appear as if there had been a sudden, late cold snap, but there hadn't.

Frank sprinted down a natural culvert and around a rocky hillside. The dirt pit that had been Lake Travis came into view.

Back in the 1940's, men had constructed a dam to create a reservoir on the Colorado River. The primary purpose of the reservoir, called Lake Travis, was to control flooding for the dramatically shifting water levels in the river. Water was managed, making it available for over a million people to drink. Lake Travis had been a large lake, often too vast to see from one side to the other. When full, Lake Travis held somewhere around 680 feet of water.

Now the lake was an empty, barren pit. Lake Travis was no

longer a lake. It looked as if a monster, too large to see from anywhere but space, had beaten a hole into the ground. A hundred foot of border lined the cracked earth in the middle of a dry basin.

At one time, islands and trees poked their heads out of the lake, but with no water the hills had been revealed and the trees had turned to pulp. Now, all that had been lake was bulldozed flat—a barren wasteland of dust that was free of all debris. The character of the lake was pushed into piles at the land-end of long unused boat ramps.

Frank looked at one such pile. It contained boulder-size rocks, root balls from trees, a broken picnic table and bones from fish and animals. He examined one set of bones more closely. Was that a human femur? He wouldn't be surprised.

He passed more boat docks that had caved into the ground, stranded on the parched, broken dirt. Boat debris littered the powdered earth nearby.

A shiny, new glass and metal structure about fifty-acres square stood in the distance. Frank jogged toward it, his feet leaving prints in plumbs of dust. Above the edge of the dirt pit that had been the lake floor, construction was near completion on Frank's baby, an enormous hydroponics farm, a long arched greenhouse, set high on concrete pilings that were solidly encased in glass and wire mesh making a 360-degree window around the farm.

Frank climbed out of the lake pit at a newly-constructed boat dock with a pier that ran from the hydroponics farm into the center of the lake. The pier was taller than the lake if it were full. He stood on the pier. He ran his hand gently, lovingly over the gray wood of the hull of a tired, old houseboat on a newly-erected dry dock. He imagined the boat refurbished, polished and gleaming. In his mind's eye, he could see it bobbing on a full lake surrounded by a verdant shoreline.

Frank pictured the lake as it had been in years past with swimmers, fisherman and boaters of all kinds, from large pleasure crafts to paddle-boarders. Frank had liked to sit lakeside at a favorite restaurant and drink Margaritas at sunset. He yearned for the yellows, purples and blues bouncing off clouds and blue water slowly turning grey as the sun hit the horizon.

An enormous cylinder, a pipe seeming to go nowhere, stretched into the lakebed and stopped at a pumping station near the middle. Viewed from space, its size belied, he might think the pipe was any sewer line. But, just like the Alaskan pipeline was built to deal with the 1973 oil crisis, this pipeline was built to deal with this current water crisis.

One hundred yards from the farm was a dilapidated, broken power station shorn up by solar power from a home panel grid. The solar power generated by the home panels had been swept up and targeted to the local hospitals, police stations and a few cooling centers with the promise that if there were excess it would be rolled back to the homes. That had yet to happen.

An assistant, Frank couldn't recall his name, a young man in dirty jeans, his thin hair pulled into a ratty ponytail, exited the building. He grinned as he walked past Frank.

"Morning, Dr. Harvey."

"Hey." Frank could tell by Pony's face that he knew that Frank didn't know his name. Frank had a dozen assistants, all of which he hired because they worked well independently. This allowed Frank to focus on what he needed to do.

"Big day," Pony said.

Frank nodded in acknowledgement. It was a big day. His heartbeat raced and not just from his jog. Frank rested his hands on his knees, as he gasped for breath.

Frank entered the back door of the hydroponics farm. Under a filtered glass skylight, row after row of dirt sat in what would soon be a mineral nutrient bath connected by a weave of intertwined gutters. Frank walked down an aisle, checking on pictures, signs that indicated what would sprout with regular water: strawberry vines, tomatoes and green beans.

In his closet of an office located within the hydroponics farm, Frank washed his face from a little filtered water in a bowl. He wet fingered his wild hair into place and then tossed the remainder of the water back into a gray water storage tank. He slipped into his nice pants and jacket before he walked out onto the pier. He rubbed the sweat from his hands on his pant legs to dry them. He was anxious, jittery.

There they were, men in suits. Frank didn't recognize the majority of the men who had gathered on the dock. He assumed that they were the big muckety-mucks of the Wagner Company — investors and board members. There was a sameness to their look. Older, principally male, dressed in garments of good taste and with a haughty, privileged expression that you might associate with old money. Of course, they were the ones who weathered the pandemic and drought the best — people with ready resources.

Pierce Wagner, a silver fox with icy blue eyes, sat apart on a deck chair, the only chair on the pier. Wagner sipped his usual aged whiskey like it was a party. He wore a blue bowling shirt that matched his eyes and drawstring cotton pants that said I'm rich enough to wear anything I want.

Charlie Broadnack refreshed Wagner's drink from a full decanter sitting on a little silver tray on the table next to the main man. While everyone else was turning into skeletons, Charlie Broadnack had grown more robust. He popped out at the middle two buttons on his standard white shirt. He tried to cover up his girth by tacking his tie in front. It didn't work.

Charlie sucked up to Wagner, pouring him his next drink, whispering into his ear, intimate, like a lover. Wagner ignored Charlie and waved over Frank.

"Man of the hour."

"Mr. Wagner," Frank responded.

"I thought I'd get to see your beautiful wife and little son today."

"Etta wasn't able to get away from the hospital."

Today was Frank's biggest success in years, in life, and Frank wasn't sure Etta had even tried to attend. He hung his head and turned his face away. He didn't want Wagner to guess that.

At four, his son Alex likely wouldn't fully understand what was happening, but he would know later. He would remember and maybe be proud of his father.

Wagner asked, "You know Charlie Broadnack?"

Frank nodded.

"We've been the best of friends for years," Charlie simpered.

Wagner nodded. He walked to the edge of the pier. "Whoo hoo," he yelled in an over-loud voice.

He nodded to Frank. Frank, in turn, nodded to Pony at a control panel, who unlocked a protective case, flipped a switch and turned a knob.

They waited, it seemed without end. Pony whispered into a battery-operated CB-type radio as he coordinated with someone at the other end of the pipeline.

Wagner rocked from foot to foot. His brows arched together into one line, his impatience growing. He was just about to open his mouth and bellow, when, slowly, water began to trickle from the pipe.

Smiles. Wagner giggled like a little girl. His mysterious men in suits also laughed and congratulated each other. And he, Frank, was the hero. Everyone wanted to stand close to him and offer him a kind word, a pat on the back or a handshake.

Frank ambled to the edge of the pier and watched as the dry lakebed absorbed the first significant drops of liquid it had seen in more than two years.

"How long will it take to fill the lake?" asked Wagner looking pensive, obviously disturbed by the slow dribble of wet. Wagner jumped back from the edge as the trickle turned into a gusher, a flood. He bolted as if he expected the water to reach out and grab him. He laughed heartily from his stomach. "Now that's what I'm talking about."

This was Frank's responsibility, his job—to create food — to save them all.

Chapter 2

At the start of the famine, farmers had cut down their drought-ruined crops. With no hope of germination of the next crop, they hadn't bothered to plant more. With no water for the animals or their pasturelands, ranchers had sent their herds to market early. They'd auctioned beef and pork at triple price, until there was no more. The farmers had plowed under their last field and the ranchers had sold their last cow to market, thus guaranteeing a famine that could not end.

As dry as it was here, that's how wet it was on the east coast. Florida over to the Louisiana Gulf Coast overflowed with water, rivers of water, floods of water, water with nowhere to go.

Frank was determined to transport the water from where they had too much to the empty Lake Travis reservoir. There was no understating what a full lake could mean to the city. Austin could be one of the last places on earth where sunshine and water came together in reasonable proportions to make food.

Frank had gone to his boss, Pierce Wagner, with his idea for a pipeline. Frank had done a lot of research into hydraulics, irrigation and water management. He had a plan for growing food, a good plan, one he knew would work.

"Aren't you a botanist? Wouldn't you need an engineer for this?" Wagner had asked.

"I'll hire if I can. I'll figure it out if I can't."

"Hasn't a pipeline been tried before?"

"It failed for political reasons, not scientific ones."

"When was that? Before the collapse?"

Frank nodded.

Frank had been stunned when the Wagner Company funded his project completely. Pierce Wagner had practically thrown money at him.

Pushed by an ambitious schedule, Frank had built his pipeline from a water restoration and reclamation plant on the Mississippi River at Shreveport, Louisiana all the way to the refurbished water storage reservoir at the Lake Travis pumping station.

Shreveport was the most populated city within eight hundred miles. It lay about three hundred miles east of Austin, across a vast expanse of parched nothing. Stragglers from what should have been upstream states including Arkansas, Oklahoma, Kansas, Missouri, Nebraska and Illinois poured into Shreveport from spaces where the ground was so sterilized that nothing would ever grow again. On the coast, the water level rose in Houston, Baton Rouge and New Orleans making those places inhospitable and so their populations escaped to Shreveport as well.

Shreveport had plenty of water and a good amount of sunshine, but food was pathetically insufficient to feed their ever-growing population. Shreveport had taken up arms to deter any further population increase. Frank had heard a rumor that thousands of people had barricaded themselves in a casino—already a small village of its own—and protected themselves with whatever force was necessary.

Wagner was the Owner and Chief Executive Officer of The Wagner Group. He inherited the business from his father when his dad died at the start of the second pandemic. That was more than a decade ago. The Wagner Group was mostly a pharmaceutical company—a company that did astronomical business with vaccines. Wagner used that money to buy up all kinds of businesses, many that did very well in the decade that followed. The think tank for which Frank worked was a private consultation firm that specialized in innovative, practical and moneymaking solutions. Most of their contracts had been with the government before the government became too weak and to disordered to stand. The United States were no longer united.

"How long will it take to fill the lake?" asked Wagner.

Frank responded to Wagner's question although the answer now seemed more obvious. "At this rate, it should take about two weeks to fill the lake's reservoir. Once the lake reaches optimal depth, we will maintain it at a constant level. We will use the water to operate the hydroponics farm. Run off, if there is any, will be released from the dam and allowed to flow down the riverbed to irrigate the gardens along the river's path."

"It's just got to keep raining on the Gulf Coast, is that right?"

"Yes sir. In this heat, the water will evaporate quickly. We'll need to keep refilling either from Shreveport or it could rain into the watershed upstream."

"Good job, Harvey. Good work, man."

Casually, Wagner handed Frank a gift-wrapped box. Frank sneaked a peek as he opened it. It was new, white running shoes.

"Thanks. I could use these." Frank hoped his face held none of the disappointment he felt. He figured there would be a reward. He hoped it would be something that Etta would like, but probably there was not enough of anything to make things right with Etta. Nothing could do that.

Frank pulled back when he noticed Charlie looking over his shoulder. Charlie was obviously thinking of things he wanted, things he thought might make him happy, but could not find. Frank doubted that there was enough of anything to make Charlie happy.

Charlie had been sporty when he and Frank first met in college. Charlie and he had rowed crew together and he spent his Sundays on the lake on a standup paddleboard. He had been agile and athletic until about a year ago when he started to flesh out. Maybe it was because he had hit thirty, but Frank thought it more likely that Charlie was eating his depression. How could he do that with food so scarce?

Frank was thirty too. He had begun to develop a belly that looked like he had swallowed a basketball until he began to run off this development by jogging five miles every day.

Frank, Charlie and Etta had just finished graduate school when the second pandemic hit. The first pandemic was Covid-19, which lasted close to four years even with working vaccines. The second pandemic was the J-flu. The J-flu hit hard and fast, wiping out whatever population was in its path.

All three had chosen career paths that were rewarded with grants and privileges in those beginning years of the collapse. Charlie studied architecture; Etta studied medicine; and Frank studied botany. These were considered highly desirable fields and they all three had made it to the end and graduated.

Charlie, Etta and he had hung out together as a threesome in college, but eventually, the time he and Etta spent together had no longer included Charlie. After the wedding, Frank still had gone rowing with Charlie on rare occasion and Etta had seen Charlie for lunch from time to time, but Frank and Etta had turned into us and Charlie was himself alone. Charlie failed to understand that.

"I'd also like to welcome you as the Wagner Group's newest Vice President." Wagner smiled.

"But I'm the Vice President," Charlie protested.

Wagner ignored Charlie. "I have an idea," Wagner said which likely meant one of his thinkers had an idea. "I was thinking it would help if we enclose the lake?"

"What do you mean?" Frank asked.

"Let's build like a big structure, a dome," Wagner suggested, "cover the lake in glass like your water farm. Yeah. That's what I want. Let's do that."

Frank glanced at Charlie, waiting for him to say something sensible. Charlie was an architect and engineer. Covering a large lake in glass would be ridiculously hard.

"I could do that." Charlie said, anxious to be the next hero.

"It's not going to be dry like this forever," Frank said. "The weather will change."

Charlie responded. "Weather report said it could be drought for years yet. And even if it rains, it must rain a lot and in the right places."

"We could have a really cool office building over there," Wagner pointed to the shoreline." He poured himself another whiskey from the decanter that had somehow grown almost empty. He was drunk. That explained a lot.

"We could build quality homes along the far shore, so that people could live in comfort, Mr. Wagner." Charlie shot Wagner a used-car-salesmen grin.

Frank knew what he really meant was quality houses so that he could live in comfort. "We don't need houses along the shore, we need food," said Frank. "An orchard would be nice."

Wagner's attention was captured by the flow of water into the lake. Some of it had started to settle into a muddy patch on the bottom near the pumping station. It splashed the feet of the dry dock at Frank's houseboat.

"Farm the land beside the lake," Wagner said.

Frank shot Charlie a winning grin.

"Build houses on the water." Wagner pointed to Frank's houseboat. "We'll create our own little Utopia."

Frank heard a distant shout of joy. Beyond the pier, on the shores of the lake, a crowd was gathering. Hundreds of people craned to get a better look as the water poured into their hopes. Armed guards held them back. A couple of little boys not much older than Alex slipped through the barricade and rolled in the fresh mud. Nobody stopped them as they yelped and giggled.

Hundreds of thousands had died in Austin alone. Billions had died around the world. After the flu pandemic, the drought and the famine, the number had been reduced by over two thirds. Still, how many of those people would get to experience Utopia?

Chapter 3

Frank left work after the presentation to Wagner and the board. He got off the train, walked about a mile down a side street toward home. Small, older frame houses were strung together by builders who assumed that people wanted to know their neighbors. These once-trendy little homes were tucked behind shops, restaurants and schools that were within easy walking distance of each other.

Frank cut the corner of the blotchy lawn of his across-the-street neighbor. Frank didn't know Hauge well. He didn't even know Hauge's first name, he was just Hauge. As Frank walked upon the patches of grass, it crunched as if someone had covered the dirt in dried cereal that broke as he trod on it.

A leafless, fifty-foot oak tree in Frank's front yard overpowered his house. Arthritic branches reached for a pale sky. The fiber cement planks siding the house were painted near the same color—like a stick of creamy butter fresh from the refrigerator. Cedar trim, a small front porch and a red door accented the house.

An overgrown prickly pear cactus covered with colorful yellow buds decorated a center flowerbed. Frank had planted the cactus when they first moved into the house. Frank thought the blooming cactus was the perfect metaphor for his wife, Etta. She sprung bright and beautiful, even in the most inhospitable environs. Frank loved the cactus and spared a portion of their water ration for it every week.

Etta slipped out the red door onto the front porch. Her pretty-as-peaches sundress wrapped her muscular thighs. Her hair, the same sienna color as the oak leaves that had fallen from the tree to the yard, cascaded down her back. She tried a tentative smile, but couldn't meet Frank's eyes.

"I missed you and Alex today," he said.

Frank watched for signs of her mood as he watered the cactus. He focused on the drips of water that clung to the fresh blooms attached to the spiny paddles as he watched her from the corner of his eyes.

"Why do you insist on watering that useless plant?" she asked.

He'd made her feel guilty and now she was mad. He felt his own heat rising.

"Are you kidding me?" he responded with no trace of amusement in his voice. "This cactus is an excellent source of food and water."

Etta looked skeptical. "You can eat that?"

"*Pollo con Nopalos*," Frank said, naming a breakfast taco she liked to eat from a local food truck they sometimes visited when it was open on Sunday mornings. The truck, a battered and rusted vehicle hadn't run in years, but the kitchen still worked. Etta had never realized that *pollo con nopalos* translated from Spanish as chicken and cactus. She wasn't much of a cook. In their marriage, that was his job.

The police whirred up the street in two newly charged electric cars. Lights flashed brightly, but there were no sirens. The cars had been repurposed from taxis found in a warehouse owned by a company that had used them in years past.

The police dragged neighbor Hauge from his house. Someone must have reported him again. Hauge had a drip system that he turned on at 3:00 in the morning to water the new plants in his backyard garden. Hauge had been fined before, first $1000, then $5000 for falsifying the number of people who lived in his home. He had done that to access more than his allotment of water.

Frank had a home garden as well. It was three times the size of Hauge's, but Frank didn't steal water. He carefully managed it. Even though Hauge was an idiot who never learned, Frank had tried multiple times to give him some tips for growing his garden which Hauge ignored. There were other ways to keep his garden alive than stealing water.

Now, the police smashed Hauge's sprinkler system and turned off his water. Hauge flinched and cried like a baby. Frank wanted to yell at him to man-up.

He and Etta had lived in this house since her mother, Henrietta, died and he had been growing and improving his garden since day one. He had built raised boxes from reclaimed wood and planted tomatoes, beans, lettuce and kale, whatever was seasonal at the time. He had solar panels on the roof of his herb porch to cut the overhead sun. For his water, he had built a gray water reclamation tower that put water from their sinks and showers through a series of filters to make it more pure for the plants. It also captured rainwater, when there was any.

The weatherman proclaimed that they had been mostly in drought for fourteen years, but that didn't mean that it never rained. Drought was a slow kill, like gradually being poisoned or radiated. In the first five years, annual rainfall had decreased from about thirty-three to sixteen inches a year. The lake had filled and drained, averaging a hold of about seventy percent of capacity.

In the beginning, most people allowed themselves to believe that everything would be fine. They recycled and patted themselves on the back as they waited for some superhero to save the day. Frank had finished high school, gone to college through grad school, met Etta and gotten married in those years of scarcity and inflation.

In the next couple years, the rain in Austin had decreased again by half, down to eight inches a year and the lake nearly evaporated away. He and Etta had moved in with her mother in what he called the years of chaos and disorder. Alex had been born then. Frank remembered feeling anxious and moody all the time, panicking for the future of his infant son. He had become obsessed with finding a way to make things better. He'd installed the solar panels, increased the size of the garden and built the large water reclamation tower.

The second pandemic, the J-flu, had lasted five years. With persistent poverty, disease and famine, reports had been that the world's population decreased from eight billion down to less than three billion. The last eight years had barely produced two inches of rain per annum. This was dystopia.

Some optimists felt like the earth had balanced itself and let a limited few survive, but he knew that, if his hydroponics farm failed, they would all surely die as other species and other civilizations had done in the distant past.

Rydell, from next door, stood at the entryway to his house clapping the hands of his two-year-old son. They watched the police cuff Hauge. The curtains moved slightly on the front window of Rydell's house.

Alex followed his mother onto the porch.

The older Rydell boy, the one about Alex's age, waved.

Alex waved back. Etta pushed him back inside, slammed the door and rushed into the street shaking her fist at Rydell. Her anguish was, for once, not aimed at Frank.

"Jebidiah," she howled as they pushed Hauge into the back of a police car.

Jebidiah. That must be Hauge's first name. No wonder that Frank didn't remember it. Who was named Jebidiah?

Etta turned on Rydell. "Did you call? You self-aggrandizing rent-a-cop?"

Rydell shrunk from the accusation.

"In times of trouble, people help each other out, not turn them in," Etta chastised.

Rydell picked up his little son, went back into his house and shut the door. He pulled the older boy from the window and closed the curtains.

Etta yelled after him. "One day you may need a friendly neighbor. What will you do then?"

The police grew jittery, unsure about Etta, so Frank pulled her back toward their porch. He felt her pull against his grip, but she came with him.

"Hauge will be okay," Frank said, thinking about the water gushing into Lake Travis. " We all will."

Frank and Etta stood on the front door landing. The police wrapped things up and whisked Hauge away. Except for the cicadas, it was still and quiet. The sidewalks were empty. The heat hung around them like a heavy, invisible blanket that made Frank feel alone, lonely. Etta took a few steps away from him.

"Mom." Alex cracked the front door and peeked out. "Can I come outside now?"

Etta nodded and laid her hand on Alex's bushy mane of blond hair, but he pulled away and wrapped an arm around one of Frank's legs.

"Hey buddy," Frank said. He loved his son, but he wasn't good with words or gestures. It felt awkward and uncomfortable to him. He didn't like having his movement restricted, but he didn't pull away. He wanted to learn to do better. "Did you have a good day?"

Etta shot him one of her looks of mock annoyance that he

knew were no longer mock, hadn't been for months. Frank hoped that if he ignored the tension one day it would go away.

Alex bubbled out a response that Frank didn't fully register.

Etta picked up the watering can that Frank had been using for the cactus. She stomped around the corner of their house and plugged in a code on the gate of the garden fence. She filled the can with water from a hose that sat coiled at the bottom of his water reclamation tower.

"What are you doing?" Frank asked, alarm in his voice. "We won't have enough water for our garden."

Etta trudged across the street with the full can. She slipped through Hauge's backyard gate and watered his plants. Frank didn't fail to notice the irony of this. There wasn't enough water for the cactus, but there was water for Hauge's miserable food plot.

"It's a garden," Etta replied. "We can't let it die."

Frank followed, but stopped at the gate and glanced around. He didn't go into Hauge's back yard, but he could see Hauge's scraggly few plants. He couldn't help but think that they didn't need this pathetic excuse for a garden any more.

"We could transplant what's still alive to our garden," he said.

"And share with Hauge?" she scoffed as if she knew that he would not.

Next door, the older Rydell boy opened his window and handed a plastic pail dripping with water out to Alex. Alex dragged it across the street to Hauge's garden, sloshing out half in his efforts. The neighbor boy giggled as he watched.

In a few hours, the sun, that searing orange disk in the cloudless sky, would sink and offer a little respite from the heat. Frank watched as many of the neighbors walked down the street. Thanks to some adjustments one of his techs had made to boost the power, a cooling center opened today in the historic post office. In an hour, the neighbors would be hidden away in a cocoon of cool. Thank you very much, he thought sarcastically. He retreated to his own garden.

Frank plopped into an Adirondack chair at the garden's edge. He could hear the concurrent songs of three or four bird types. An array of different bugs came out. He hoped that Etta would join him, so that they could watch Alex play in the dirt the way they used to when Alex was a toddler.

Etta and Alex entered the back yard. She again filled the watering can, but she didn't move off with it. She stood in her beautiful dress and stared at him.

Electricity, not water, had become the first casualty of the drought. At first, power had been cut one day a week between 3:00 and 5:00 in the afternoon when people were supposedly at work. Then the blackout had been expanded to every afternoon — the afternoon blackout. Finally, everyone was without power almost all the time. Power was provided in short rolling bursts only.

Alex left the hose dribbling after he filled his second pail of water. Frank went over to turn it off. When he returned to his chair, Alex moved between Frank's legs. Alex obviously wanted to be lifted, so he did.

Frank thought that Alex was beautiful — his bush of blond curls, his pouty lips and he had these over-huge green eyes with stunningly long lashes. This little being was his to protect. Watching over Alex fortified him. Holding Alex with his warm skin, sweet smell and soulful stares petrified him. From the first moment that Frank had witnessed Alex's little head push into the world, Frank had been affected by a surreal sense of panic.

"Alex, you're four now. You're too big to sit in my lap."

Another annoyed look from Etta. "He just wants a hug. He hasn't seen you all day."

"Anyway," he said. "It shouldn't matter soon. The pipeline's up and running now." Frank waited for her to remember and respond to his big news, but she didn't. He couldn't help feeling hurt and disappointed.

Etta spoke to Alex. "Do you want to see if Jared wants to go to the cooling center with us?" Even though she knew his answer she turned to Frank and asked, "Do you want to come?"

"I have work to do." You know, saving the city and all. No cocoon of cool for him. "Tomorrow, I'll transfer Hauge's plants to our garden," he said. "We can better keep them alive here."

Etta nodded. She left the full pails of water for him to deal with.

Frank went into the house and shut the door.

Frank tried to work in the half-light and eerie shadows made by his elderly laptop, but he couldn't concentrate and the batteries were draining. Two lamps at either end of the sofa snapped on. Frank blinked a few times adjusting to the light. The afternoon blackout was over. He stood and looked around his house. He plugged in his computer to charge.

Frank shared a modest three bedroom, two bath with his wife and son. It was a character house: old, painted a little too brightly and filled with furniture from another time, mostly Etta's maternal grandmother's time. The walls were covered in photographs of Etta's family. There were posed wedding shots of her grandparents on both sides, of her parents and of them, but most of the pictures were snaps of family life as she and her twin sister Lola grew up. Etta was the third generation of her family to live in this house.

They had named it the Jersey Pandemic or just J-flu for short because the first case was identified in Newark. Etta's mother had called for Etta to come home to say her goodbyes to her grandfather who had the J-flu, but by the time they arrived, he had been dead for two days. That was the first time Frank had smelled lingering rot. Etta's mother had not been able to obtain overtaxed mortuary services. That was before the death carts and mass burnings. Etta's Mom was sick herself with grief and she had died a few days later. Frank had dug one wide hole in the back yard. He'd wrapped them each in a cotton sheet with a damask pattern from off the bed and he had buried Etta's mom and dad side by side. Frank had wanted to cry, but instead he ground down his feelings between his gritted teeth.

A watercolor loomed in the hallway centered over Etta's grandmother's teak entry table. Frank stared at this picture. In it, Etta was five months pregnant, her belly rounded like a soccer ball under her casual dress. Alex, then not quite age three years old, was attached to Etta's leg. One of Etta's hands lightly rested on Alex's tousled mane of hair. Frank, at Etta's other side, rested his hand on Etta's belly.

Frank set his computer aside, stood, and took the painting off the wall. He stomped into the bedroom, where he tucked it into Etta's grandmother's teak wardrobe.

Etta bounced into the house, bright and animated. "There's light in our house," Etta said.

She and Alex were both excited from their evening out. They sang in rounds. It was a song that Etta's mother sang to her as a child, something about bells and fairies.

From the hall, Frank heard Etta call. "Where's the family portrait?" Frank knew that to Etta this picture represented the last time they were truly happy as a family.

Frank collided with Etta at the bedroom door. "I can't look at it," Frank said sounding angry and hopeless even to himself. He slammed the door in his wife's face.

"Franklin. I can't do this anymore." Etta's voice sounded sad. "Do you hear me?" He said nothing. "I think it's time we separate."

Frank opened the door. He leaned on the doorjamb.

Neither said a thing. A single tear slid down Frank's cheek. Etta pulled Frank into her arms. She stroked the back of his neck.

"We did our best," she said.

"I know."

"Stay until you have somewhere to go."

"I think I'll have a place soon."

Etta jumped back. Raised her voice a little. "You already have a new place?" She looked bitter, but got herself under control. "Where?"

"I bought an old houseboat. It's not livable right now. I'm going to fix it up."

"Does it have a bedroom for Alex?"

"It has berths, four of them. Alex will think that's fun, like bunk beds."

"Promise me," she said. "Promise me you won't cut him out of your life."

"I promise."

"He needs you."

"I know."

Etta gave him that annoyed, disbelieving look again. He loved her so much.

Chapter 4

Glistening water lapped the sides of a houseboat and lifted it so that it was even with the slip. Each glossy surface of the boat shone with new paint and varnished wood. Frank, Etta and six-year-old Alex admired the boat from the pier.

"It's beautiful," Etta said. A slight breeze lifted the front strands of Etta's copper hair.

The last two years had brought many changes. The lake was full. A hydraulic pump gurgled under the surface, like a water feature that was constantly running. A dozen houseboats had joined Frank's in stalls along the wharf. So many more were planned so that the pier had turned a corner and been extended almost to the dam. The hydroponics farm was at the beach end of the dock. The shore was lined with waist-tall fruit trees, each surrounded by a circle of dark rich mulch. A footpath twisted through the immature trees.

At the edge of the lake, two more edifices were in progress. One was called simply the Wagner Building. When completed, it would house a combination of apartment residences and offices. Beyond that, a new and improved power plant had been framed out.

Over the whole thirty plus square miles of lake and surrounding shore, cranes lifted a fancy metal grid and welded each piece into place. Sparks made a light show in the western sky.

Frank jumped from the pier to the houseboat's deck and held out his hand, but Etta ignored it. Etta helped Alex over and then stepped onto the deck by herself. They stood under an overhang that shaded the deck from the sun.

"The boat I bought was a wreck. Turned out to be more rotten than I could repair. I had to scrap it. So, Wagner gave me this new one."

"He just gave it to you?" Etta asked.

"I'm important to him." Frank said. "He's pleased with my work."

Etta looked up. "What's all that metal work?"

"A dome. The biggest problem in a drought is evaporation. The dome will keep the moisture in the lake, like a giant terrarium. That will help us with farming."

Etta rested her fingers on his forearm. "I'm so proud of you, Franklin. Look at what you've done."

He felt his face flush. "Not me alone," he said humbly. He turned away and opened a door. "Come see the inside."

The front door off the swimming deck opened into a common area, a combination living room dominated by a long window, sofa under it, an office to one side, dining at an island and an open kitchen. It was nice, sleek and made great use of the available space.

"Very modern," Etta said. "And the berths?"

Frank pointed left toward a door. "An actual bedroom and this sofa is plenty big for sleeping. The Wagner Group has restricted the size of houseboats on the lake to five hundred square feet, so it's all very compact."

"Why do they get to say?"

Frank resented that comment. "I guess money buys some privileges," he shrugged. "All the living spaces are regulated to a common size. Wagner thinks that will help to avoid conflict." This wasn't the direction he wanted this conversation to go. He wanted Etta to be impressed.

Etta took a careful step back. "It is nice and seems plenty big enough for you and Alex when he comes to visit."

"It will be more beautiful inside the dome when all the vegetation matures." He spread his arms showing off the view from the bay window, just like a realtor. "See the lake. Imagine all the green growing on shore. You'll like that."

"I will?" Etta asked in surprise.

"I refurbished this boat for the three of us."

"Alex and I intend to stay in our house. It's near my hospital and his school. All our friends are in easy walking distance. Same with the park, stores and the like."

"There isn't anything in the stores. The safest place is going to be ..."

"...In this sterile, isolated cell?"

"I thought it was lovely. I thought you were proud," Frank snapped.

Etta released Alex's hand which she hadn't let loose since they stepped on the boat. "What do you think, Honey? Want to visit Daddy here sometimes?"

Alex paced the length of the floor in response. It didn't take long. He hopped in a circle, showing off the small size of the space. "Can we sail the boat out into the middle? Alex asked. "Will you teach me to swim?"

"It's not a sailing boat," Frank said.

"Daddy's going to live here, Sweetie," Etta turned away from Alex and spoke softly, "but I never will."

Chapter 5

The sun reflected off the mirrored surface of a new four-story glass and metal building located at the lake's edge. It was one of only two multi-story buildings planned to be inside the biodome, the other being the power station. Frank raised his hand to shield his eyes as he looked up at it. A sign announced that the new edifice would house both offices and apartments for Wagner's employees. Frank thought it was hideous and cliché with its science fiction lines.

He whisked through the automatic glass door. The light changed from warm to cool. In an atrium, he was dwarfed by tall angles and wide spaces.

He saw Wagner in the spacious lobby on the border of a team of people who wore matching navy tee shirts and gray sweats. They surrounded a mat where a hand-to-hand exhibition match was in progress. Most of the observers were big, burly men, thumping the Wagner logo on their chests, but there were also a few women, thumping in their own way, not loud and primal like the men, but quiet in a powerful way. Everyone yelled encouragement to someone or the other.

Frank walked up and stood beside Wagner.

"Private security force," Wagner said. "Might be more than a few people who'll want what we have."

Frank watched the match. It was a man and a woman, both young and pretty, especially her. Her thick, wavy hair flowed like a cape as she spun. She taunted the young man, and then whirled out of his way when he lunged. She clocked him a good blow in the ribs, hard, but not hard enough to bruise given the thick gloves she wore.

"That's Detective Anne Roget. She's quick on her feet and smart. Stubborn, that one, but patient. That's why I hired her." Wagner smiled. "And that's why I put my money on her."

"Too late to get in on that?" Frank quipped.

Wagner huffed.

Her male opponent was tall and lean. He had long, sinewy muscles that responded to his every want. His features were classic, like a Roman soldier of old. He gleamed at her.

"Bring him to his knees, Anne," Wagner called.

A shot was delivered, another taken. Back and forth. Sweat slicked their faces and arms. The fight was serious, but they looked like they were really enjoying it.

The female detective circled her opponent, never breaking eye contact. She struck a blow, grazing his shoulder. He went with the movement, swung around and kicked out her feet. She went down hard on her back, hardly making solid contact before she attempted to scramble back up. He straddled her, grabbed her hands and pinned them with a sturdy grasp over her head. She struggled, wriggled.

The hooting and hollering of the observers rose to a fever pitch. Wagner yelled along with the rest of them. "Get out from under him Anne," he yelled. "It's a fight, not sex."

The man transferred both of Anne's hands into one of his. She resisted, but not much. She relaxed into the floor. He ran his free hand down her arm, her side, and let it rest next to her breast. Then he kissed her hard and she responded. She pulled one arm free and wrapped it around his neck. She added one leg, swinging it around his back.

"Fucking newlyweds," Wagner yelled. He pulled a clump of bills from his pocket and shoved them into the hand of a nice-looking kid, maybe sixteen or seventeen, with an arrogant smile. "Somebody throw some water on them." Wagner clapped the young man on the shoulder.

Anne used the power of her legs to flip the man onto his back. It was her turn to straddle him. He was breathing heavy but no longer fighting back.

Wagner beamed. He pulled the clump of bills back. "She's got some fight left in her yet," he said.

Wagner took Frank's arm and guided him toward his office. Frank suspected that Wagner was making his escape before the man flipped Anne and she was down again, however neither one of the newlyweds acted ready to give up.

Frank followed Wagner to a first floor space dominated by a glass wall. The room they were in was primarily an office. A palatial wooden desk dominated the wall of windows with a pair of comfy chairs in a little conversational area to one side. There was a Murphy bed Frank doubted was ever opened. The kitchenette was more a bar than a kitchen. Shelves of liquor bottles decorated the back wall. Wagner had crowded the room with all the beautiful things for which he could find space.

Frank stood at the window thinking how odd it seemed that Wagner didn't select the top floor for himself. The penthouse. That was Wagner's style. Wagner had a view of the hydroponics farm and the orchards going up along the shore under the almost completed biodome.

"That?" Frank pointed to a massive structure on the east shore.

"Light rail train station," Wagner said.

"Inside or out?" Frank asked.

"It will be outside the gateway to the dome. The trains run on electricity. The tracks will be powered by heliostatic solar panels attached to the roof of the dome. The solar panels adjust so that they face the sun all day long."

Frank said, "Good idea." He had to give Charlie and his team of builders some props. This whole city on the water was quite an accomplishment.

According to Wagner's own rule, every Wagner employee's space was to be a standard 500 square feet, but Frank noticed a hidden door behind a bookshelf standing slightly ajar. Behind the door, he saw a much bigger room.

Through the gap in the hidden door, Frank caught a glimpse all the way to a far wall of windows. It was a living room, long and elegant, decked out in a modern style, circular sofa with two ottoman coffee tables and yet another bar. On the far wall were five doors leading to additional spaces beyond.

Wagner casually slid the door shut with his hip as he steered Frank's attention back toward the view from the office window.

"There's your hydroponics farm and you can see the extent of the planting along the shoreline from here," he pointed out.

With the amount of resources that Wagner poured into these projects, Frank didn't really care about Wagner breaking his own rules. He easily sent his attention where Wagner directed it and pretended not to have seen the hidden door behind his bookcase, but he wondered about it. A man with a secret door likely had other secrets too.

"It's going well. This time next year there should be lots more food." He turned to Wagner, "but it still won't be enough, you know." Wagner looked solemn. "That's what I wanted to talk to you about today."

"You have a plan? Is there a way to make more?" Frank asked.

"Not that I know of, but I do have a plan."

Wagner waited as if expecting Frank to guess it, but Frank didn't have a clue. Finally, Wagner turned to the window and looked out toward the dome's open gateway.

Frank felt his pulse jump and his face turn crimson. He understood. He knew the words Wagner would say before they came out of his mouth.

"You said it yourself. We can't save everyone."

Chapter 6

Stick trees swayed in a sudden gust. The weather had cooled off, moved toward winter, making it less unpleasant to be outdoors, so people forgot it still hadn't rained. People had adapted to the food and water rationing and to the electric blackouts.

Frank brought his son and the older Rydell boy from next door to the park. Alex and his friend were six years old. Frank had brought a basketball as he thought that was what they might enjoy. Instead, Frank watched Alex as he played some weird game with the Rydell kid. Alex was at the top of the monkey bars while Rydell was at the bottom. Rydell chased Alex from the ground as Alex climbed in and over the monkey bars to stay away. Rydell shrieked with laughter each time Alex scurried away from him. Alex hooted in turn, a pure, carefree amusement lighting his eyes. It made Frank snicker as well.

Frank could see the biodome in the distance. He could not tell from this far, but he knew that today a team of workers scrambled over the top of the dome installing the solar panels. The new and improved electric grid would come on in about a week and the light rail would soon be up and running.

He lived on his houseboat full time now. At the divorce proceedings when the judge asked if there was any chance of reconciliation, Frank had surprised everyone by saying "yes."

Etta was the only person who had ever looked at him with eyes full of love. Even when she'd felt angry or disappointed or alone, she'd stop to consider what would be the loving choice and do that. He told the judge how much he wished he'd stopped to reconsider the words that flew out of his mouth and could never be retrieved. The judge had put the proceedings on hold for nine months while he and Etta went to therapy. It had not worked.

Frank touched the papers tucked inside his jacket next to his heart. In the end, he could not make Etta do what she would not do. He had signed the papers.

Frank had tried spending the day with Alex at the houseboat, but he had to admit he was at a loss for what to do with Alex there. Frank had bought toys and games, but Alex just didn't seem interested, so they'd come to the park near their, now Etta's, house where he could play with his friends from the neighborhood.

There was no play space under the dome. Wagner wouldn't allow it. Every inch was for working, living or planting. So, the inhabitants tended to stay in their own honeycomb within the hive. Frank missed his family. He missed living at home.

Tall and slim, Etta walked toward them. She wore a long trench coat, like a gunslinger. It floated around her body on the cool breeze, flapping open now and again to show her long legs. Tights kept her legs warm. Today, she wore a worsted dress under her coat. She liked dresses and wore them well. She had on a felt hat that covered all but the ends of her long, russet curls.

Etta carried a large brocade shoulder bag. She set it on the picnic table where Frank sat as he kept watch over Alex. Etta laid her hand over Frank's for just a moment. He felt the warmth of it through his glove.

"Alex. It's time for lunch. Have Jared come join us," she called to their son, her breath forming puffs of icy fog.

Jared. Frank had tried to remember the Rydell boy's first name all morning. Jared Rydell.

Etta opened her bag and pulled several plastic containers from inside.

Alex swung out from the top of the monkey bars. He did a flip, but landed on his feet. Both Frank and Etta sucked in a gasp, but Frank was proud at the same time. "Where did he learn to do that?" Frank asked.

"I don't know."

They looked in wonder as their son ran to them. "Stay for lunch, Franklin."

He wanted to. Badly. Instead he pulled the manila envelope that contained the divorce papers from his inside pocket and set them on the table between them. "I can't." He kissed her cheek and walked away.

Chapter 7

With the focus on the struggle to survive, development in technology had been frozen for more than a decade. There had been no phone upgrades, no improved models of tablets, laptops or desktops. These and things like fans, toasters and microwave ovens were thrown out when they broke. There had been no purpose in designing or developing anything new.

But now, thanks to Frank's pumping station, the power plant was back online and electricity was more readily available. They hadn't yet found people skilled in the all the technology of the past, but still he couldn't help but have a bit of hope for the normalcy to come.

Frank ambled over to the Wagner building to pick up his new toy. Wagner's scientists had been able to develop an uber-smart computer/phone from the unrealized designs of a genius inventor named Kolli Veddka.

Last year, Frank had managed to acquire a beta-version of this device for his son's sixth birthday. It wasn't sophisticated. It was clunky, hand-held and didn't have many security features. When Frank had asked what to get, Etta said that Alex really wanted one. Frank couldn't imagine why as there was barely anyone to connect with. But then, Alex had called Frank's computer, an old 2013 MacBook Pro, to thank him. On the call, Etta had said it was the best gift Frank had ever gotten for his son.

Frank would have to buy Alex this newest version on his ninth birthday coming up soon.

A techie made a cut into the fleshy part between Frank's thumb and index finger. He embedded a tiny network device called The Nomad under Frank's skin.

The Nomad used any available surface as a monitor. It created a small image that could be seen in the palm of your hand, but with a flick of your wrist toward a solid surface, the image became as large as you like. The Nomad guessed whether to make the image 2D, 3D or 4D. Text and figures usually came up 2D, but photos, videos and calls usually popped up 3D. 4D could be called up to see inside two-dimensional spaces. With a word command, you could easily switch between each.

The Nomad used artificial intelligence to perform an unlimited number of tasks. It was especially known for its security features that used a combination of a heart rate monitor, face recognition and voice recognition to authenticate its user. The Wagner group added an employee ID number on top of that for accessing work products. The Nomad's recognition protocol was sophisticated, recognizing an unlimited number of patterns and languages.

Frank knew that Etta had known Kolli Veddka before the second pandemic and therefore she had told him a bit of his history. Veddka had left behind a good job in California to become one of the original members of the Wagner Company's think tank.

When the Wagner Company first created the think tank, it was primarily a pharma company. The whole business was concentrated on vaccines, likely as a response to Covid 19, and then later the J-flu. Pierce Wagner expanded the focus in many directions, looking for solutions to many of the world problems that had impacted him.

Kolli Veddka had left the think tank under strained circumstances, apparently having different opinions than Pierce Wagner about who should profit from his inventions. Veddka had thought the products of his research should be open source, available to everyone to share. Wagner had believed work product was his own to control. Veddka took twenty-two members of the think tank with him when he left the sterile environment provided by Wagner. They'd set up shop in the basement of a defunct research lab and health clinic.

Frank had heard that at least twenty of the think tank members had died, maybe from of a new virulent strain of influenza, maybe something else. Frank didn't know exactly what had happened.

Not wanting the legal fight, Veddka had left behind the inventions he'd developed for the Wagner Company when he left, including all his designs and code, but if anyone thought him or herself smart enough to alter his work, they instead found bugs and traps, putting all the code that supported the most important aspects of their lives at risk.

Veddka had disappeared, but sightings of him continued to pop up like an Elvis with a savior complex.

So, nobody touched the code. Ever. It wasn't long before no one knew how.

Scientists instead developed the Repository from Veddka's sketchy designs. The Repository was an object-oriented compilation of their most precious computer code. It was like a library for computer programs, a storage space to ensure that they always had a backup from which to make a copy.

Wagner had scoured universities for the next Kolli Veddka, but universities had suffered too. With the J-flu, many public institutions had closed and parents had opted for home schooling or online programs where face-to-face contact was not required.

Wagner's search had found Frank. That's how Frank, and soon after Charlie, had come to work for Wagner. Etta had told Frank she didn't want him work for Wagner, that he gave her the creeps and she had been unhappy with his choice. She wouldn't work for him. Instead, she had picked a nearby hospital where she thought she could do more good.

Frank lifted his hand. He felt a slight tingling as the device calibrated to his body. The tech showed him how to set it up for his personal preferences and contacts.

Frank had gotten hold of a beta-version of the Nomad for his son, still he hadn't thought to get one for himself. It was Wagner who provided all his executive team with his latest investment. Frank realized in that moment what a gift the Nomad was for him as well.

"Locate Alex Harvey," Frank gave the Nomad a try.

Alex and Etta's image shot out from the device into his palm. Frank flicked his wrist and the image flickered around the room until he aimed it at a wall. The 3D image compensated for the background and made the tech transparent as well as a standard screen hanging on the wall. It made the background appear to disappear.

The Nomad found Alex via a chip in his hand. Frank guessed that he was too late to buy the latest version for Alex. He already had one.

It then linked one of thousands of webcams, security cameras and satellite receivers that had been activated everywhere around the city since electric power had been restored.

In the Nomad's 3D image, Etta and Alex exited a square, industrial building, pausing to chat with a few people. As far as he knew, Etta didn't know these people. It wouldn't matter to her whether or not she did.

The tech handed Frank a small earpiece. Frank inserted it into his ear so that he could hear the conversations around Alex quite well.

Frank zoomed in and stared until Etta and Alex turned and parted company from the strangers.

"Inspired," he said.

As he left the building, Frank thought about how much he wanted to thank Wagner, let him know what this connection to his son meant.

Frank needed certain basic information about a person to set him or her as one of the selections, but it didn't take much. He set up Wagner as one of his contacts on the Nomad.

"Locate Pierce Wagner," he told the device.

Frank opted to leave the image on his palm to afford himself a little privacy. If Wagner had been in his office, there would have been more security, but Wagner walked through a public area, one of Frank's new orchards, chatting with Charlie Broadnack. They looked chummy and casual, so Frank decided to virtually join them.

He guessed the password for linking to Wagner's sound at the least confidential level, got it on his first try. The password was Parker, as in Parker Heritage Bourbon, Wagner's favorite drink.

"Earcuff on," Frank told a small jewel attached to his outer ear that connected to his Nomad. As he listened, he began to pick up Wagner's conversation. Frank guessed that they all would have to get used to being surveilled again, having their private lives monitored.

"It has to be secret or there might be panic," Wagner said.

"When?"

"After people settle at home. Seven, maybe eight o'clock tonight."

Someone walked by.

Frank wasn't certain yet what this conversation meant, but he was sure he didn't want to be caught eavesdropping on it.

"I've bought a luxury tower downtown for our outside needs," Wagner said. "I want you to renovate and redesign it."

"You want me to work outside?" Charlie had a bit of panic in his voice.

"Work, Live. Yes. You'll have all the resources you need."

"But." Charlie was still hesitant. "Have I done something wrong? Am I being punished?"

Being around Charlie was driving Frank insane, so he'd told Wagner that he might move back outside after his work on establishing the farm was finished. Wagner was clear he wanted Frank on the inside. He had told Frank he would take care of Charlie. Frank wondered if this was Wagner taking care of it.

"The gate will be locked for everyone?" Charlie asked Wagner. "No one will get in or out."

Wagner responded, "There might be a few exceptions," he paused, "but very few."

"Just to be clear, I'm an exception," Charlie said.

Frank had felt it for months, but refused to acknowledge it. He'd seen it on his spreadsheets. He should have known this was coming. There wasn't enough food for everyone so today was the day they were cutting off the outsiders. Frank's first worry was for Etta and Alex.

Chapter 8

Frank ran to the hospital. He looked through the crowd of sick and injured to find Etta. There she was.

Sometimes Etta's grace hit Frank like a jolt from a stun gun. His heart raced from the impact, pounding blood to all his senses until she appeared to slow down, as if they had moved from an action scene in a movie to a romance scene, all slo-mo and sensuous.

Etta instructed the nurse at the end of the hall. She turned as elegant as a ballet dancer, saw him and smiled, actually smiled when she noticed the amazed look on his face. He knew it had not been there in a while. Etta walked with poise, seemed to float, down the hall toward him. He had trouble swallowing. He missed her so much.

Frank had met Etta when she was nineteen. Charlie Broadnack had first spotted her on the mall outside the Sciences building when they were at the University of Texas. Charlie always said that he called dibs, but if he did, Frank had never heard him. He couldn't have heard anything over the pounding in his ears.

Etta had completed an expedited medical program offered by a downtown hospital — the purpose of which had been to develop doctors quickly. He and Etta had gotten married just after graduation. When her father became sick, they had moved into Etta's parents' house to help care for him. During her residency at Seton Hospital and Frank's first year with the Wagner group, Alex had been born.

Etta was a busy doctor when she had become pregnant for the second time. She had gotten a severe kidney infection with that one. An infection that had caused pre-term labor that was too early for the baby to survive.

Now, she practically ran this hospital by herself. She had found administrators, nurses and assistants, but she was the sole surviving doctor.

His distress must have showed. When she reached him, Etta gave him a peck on the cheek.

"Hello Franklin."

"I need to talk to you. Can we take a little walk?"

She seemed to want to protest, but could not turn away from his somber expression. She nodded.

Frank took her arm as they walked outside. They crossed the street and walked to a little green space that was not green and did not have much space. Frank's hand slipped down her arm and he gently held Etta's hand. She let him. There were a good number of people on the path, so Frank guided her away from them.

"Frank, what is this?" Etta asked not impatiently.

"You know I love you and Alex," he said. She started to protest, but he rushed on before she could. "I've always believed that we were meant to be together and that we would find our way back to each other in time, but time has run out."

"Love was never the issue..." She interrupted herself when she heard the important part of the sentence. "What do you mean time has run out?"

"They plan to lock the gate on the dome tonight. I don't know what that will mean, but it can't be good. I want you and Alex to move onto the houseboat with me before that happens."

"But, you'll be locked in."

"I need you to move in with me. I want you to move in."

Etta gave off vibrations of confusion, real physical waves of angst. "But" was all she managed to say.

"I can't protect you outside the dome. There will be nothing I can do."

Etta's expression was complex and conflicted, but then she paused. A look of kindness and understanding crossed her face. She knew what he was thinking even when he did not.

"The baby was so premature. Her lungs weren't fully formed."

"And there was nothing I could do," he said.

Tears filled Etta's eyes. "It wasn't your fault."

"Meet me at the train station's coffee shop at the dome's gateway at six o'clock tonight."

She didn't say anything for a long time, but then, "I'll think about it."

Twilight. The sun started its slow path down the edge of the curved, almost transparent biodome. An unlit grid of electric lights covered its glass and metal surface. The heliostat mirrors attached to a tall tower turned toward the fading sun.

Within the dome, humidity gathered at the concave tip of the dome's interior surface. Moisture fell like a gentle rain on the lake below. Drops twinkled in the soft light on the rooftops of the houseboats that dotted the pier.

Above the biodome's gateway blinked a Jumbotron. The sign said, "The Wagner Company Food Security Project" and below that the claim "Food for All."

Outside the gate, Frank paused for breath on the platform of the train station that was built to connect the dome's residents to the people and places of the city. An agitated crowd pushed against the dome's open gateway, trying to get inside. He guessed that Wagner's little secret was out.

Wagner's uniformed security officers, including the fighter-girl and her new husband from the main building lobby, physically forced themselves between the people outside and the gateway to the dome. The officers pushed back the crowd as best they could.

"Food for everyone," Fighter-girl yelled. "It says so right there," she indicated the giant sign, but she didn't seem to believe it any better than the masses forming at the gate. Likely, she was just trying to calm people down.

Frank, wild-haired, wild-eyed, ran down the crowded deck of the light rail train station toward the little coffee shop where he'd asked Etta and Alex to meet him. With each step he grew more certain she had not come.

But they were there. Etta's gauzy red dress the only pop of color on the train station deck. Frank exhaled a breath of relief. In the station's coffee shop, Alex wiggled on his chair watching the commotion, wanting to be a part of it. Etta took his hand and stood when Frank caught sight of them.

Frank ran against the tide. He pushed his way through, shoving the natives aside as he went.

"Etta, we only have a few minutes. Come on."

Alex clutched for Etta as Frank lifted him into his own arms.

"No," Alex protested. "I'm too big to be carried." Alex struggled from Frank's arms.

Frank grabbed Etta's hand and pulled her toward the open gateway. As they got closer, Etta resisted. "I'm not sure." Etta took Alex's hand and pulled him to her.

Frank gave her another tug. "What?"

"Franklin, I don't think I can."

"Don't be silly. Look around you."

"There aren't any kids in there. I want Alex to have friends."

"But food. I want Alex to have food."

Etta didn't budge. "Stay with us," she suggested.

"Please," Frank begged. "I can't help you out there." Frank stopped still within the chaos. "I can't help anyone. The farm is inside."

Beyond Frank and Etta, a desperate man struggled with a male security guard in his panicked attempt to gain access to the dome. Frank recognized the guard, the newlywed.

A warning tone blared.

Lights in the grid that covered the outside of the curved surface of the dome blinked red, making the dome look like a giant electrified golf ball. First, one section of the dome lights turned white. In a few minutes, another section changed color. It progressed from there.

The desperate man pushed the officer who fell against the electrified dome surface just as the lights changed from red to white in that section. Current coursed through the officer. He fell into spasms.

Etta covered Alex's eyes.

Frank heard a wail, a primal scream. Fighter-girl charged toward her downed husband from one direction as Etta rushed toward him from another.

"I'm a doctor," Etta said as she checked the fallen man's vitals. "What's your name?" she asked Fighter-girl in a calm voice.

"Anne. Anne Roget," Fighter-girl said by habit as she fell to her knees.

Etta gave Alex's hand to Anne. "Don't let go," she warned.

Anne held Alex's hand tightly, until he yowled and pulled it away.

Etta worked to save the officer. Etta pulled back his head and breathed into his mouth. She pushed with all her weight onto the man's chest.

Anne ran her hand across her husband's forehead and hair. "Everything's fine. Everything's going to be okay." She tried to sound reassuring, but couldn't make herself hit the right note.

Horrified, Frank looked around. "Etta, we have to go." Etta had tuned him out. Frank couldn't get through to her. "Etta. Now."

One section and all the gateway lights would turn steady and white. Stay or go? In less than a minute, the gate would be locked. In a panic, Frank ran toward the biodome gateway before it was too late.

Frank thought he heard Alex running after him as he shot toward the entrance of the dome. ID badge at the ready, Frank jumped through the gate just in time. Inside, he trembled. He couldn't catch his breath. He struggled to gain his feet, but his knees wouldn't support him.

"Oh God," he said as he finally stood.

Frank searched for Etta and Alex through the dome's clear glass structure. Etta was where he had left her. She continued to perform artificial respiration on the downed officer. He saw Etta's realization that Alex was not in sight. Frank searched, looking for Alex through the dome's transparent structure.

Frank felt insane as he searched the crowd looking for his young son. Soon, he spotted Alex on the outside.

Through the hazy surface, Alex stood with his hands on his hips in a look that was unbelievably hostile and confrontational for an six-year old boy. He stood still and rigid.

Frank had to turn away.

Part II

Chapter 9

Year 2045

All Alex saw was a tangle of legs as he chased his father's retreating path. Alex yelled at the top of his lungs. "Daddy wait." But his father ran away from him. "Wait for me. I want to come," Alex screamed.

He lost sight of his father's pant leg in an instant. Alex weaved and pushed through the crowd. Soon, he realized that he was lost and alone.

He despaired in this memory. Alex opened his red-rimmed eyes. Now sixteen, he was tall and lean like his mother with taut, long muscles. He'd shorn his hair close to the head, his being too much like his father's. The near-baldness set off his hazel eyes. He wore brown, the color of dirt, against the trend to wear light, sun-friendly fabrics. His sunglasses were a bit too small to be trendy and emphasized his overlarge ears.

Alex crouched on the biodome train station roof. He fidgeted, defeating his desire to blend with stillness against an old exhaust fan on the flat roof and escape notice of the nearby security camera. His fingers beat out a rhythm on his bended knee.

The roof offered him a wide view in every direction, but he focused instead on a small sketchpad on which he had drawn the scene, the tangle of legs he remembered as his father abandoned him.

The sun rose over the convex edge of the dome. It shone brighter and brighter until the sky was white. Waves of heat rippled off the dome's thick glass surface and beat down on Alex's unprotected face. Alex touched his exposed nose and put on a reflective billed cap, like ones used for baseball in days past that also covered his shorn head.

Through the skin of the dome, Alex saw his father's houseboat as it bobbed lazily at a wooden pier that connected the train station on one shore and the dam at the other end. It was wedged in between similar houseboats, all attractive and well maintained. Under the transparent surface of the dome, it looked blurred at the edges, like a fisheye photo.

Alex watched his father step out onto the swimming deck of the houseboat. He looked fresh and cool in a white tee shirt just slightly paler than his skin tone, shorts and white running shoes. He jogged in place until he found his pace and then began a slow run down the pier toward the shore. He jumped a couple feet from the pier to the hiking trail that wound through a peach orchard, ripe with fruit, past the honeybee sanctuary surrounded by redbud trees.

His father wasn't fat, his morning jogs took care of that, but like most the insiders, he was well fed. In a minute, his dad was around the corner and out of Alex's sight.

Outside the dome, a scant population lived in a city fallen into ruin. Dust floated like a dark cloud over decaying structures. In the distance, the ground was literally ablaze. Wild fires raged across desert brush as the wind pushed the flames, smoke and ash toward once-nice homes that were being reclaimed by the elements. A cargo plane swept across the landscape and when it reached the fire, it dropped a load of red retardant.

At the dome's entrance, the starving loitered, skinny as twigs, moving slowly, like zombies. There were just a few of the starving left, not nearly so many as the scary-huge numbers in the past. They banged against the clear barrier that separated them from food and water until ultimately they sank down the dome's side to die.

Each morning, a city police crew came to gather the fallen. They came with a hand-drawn cart. The dead were too many to waste precious resources such as gasoline or even electricity just to haul the bodies to a funeral pyre and burn them. He wondered that they wasted the match.

When work first began on the dome, it had become clear that food was going to be grown inside. People came from everywhere, refugees from drought or flood, already skin and bones. At first, the Wagner Company selected certain people with good skills that the guards let inside, but soon the policy changed. The guards responded with batons and stun guns, making it clear that the food was not for them — the outsiders.

If you lived outside, you had to have an ID with a permanent address on file from before the dome was built to obtain food from a Wagner Company kiosk. This created a new kind of middle class, people who owned property, but had nothing else.

The rush of strangers from unknown places had stopped. Maybe that meant that there were no more people on this part of the globe. He couldn't believe that something as minor as an address would have deterred anyone. Maybe Wagner's private police kept them away from the town and the dome. Maybe the starving at the dome's edge were the few who managed to get through.

Alex had a name for each one of the cops who responded to the death calls. He knew how they treated the dead. Handsome, with his over-large eyes and insincere smile, treated them like dog shit left under his shoe. Tiny was bright, happy and just one foot taller than a Christmas elf. She labored and grunted under their unyielding weight.

Only Vixen cared. She took a minute and held the hand of each person, maybe saying a prayer wishing them on their way. She checked for ID and called them by name. She lifted them gently onto the stretcher and waved them goodbye as they disappeared in the death cart to the fires.

Alex drew a pencil sketch of the man Vixen held in her arms. It wasn't as gruesome as it sounded. Alex tried to find something distinctive about his appearance. The man had long, kinky hair and a rodeo belt buckle. Alex tried to create an image of how he must have looked before the Famine. It just seemed wrong to him to reduce the dead to ash without any kind of record of who they might have been. One day, his family might come looking and Alex's drawing might be the only record of what had happened to him.

From the roof of the train station, Alex watched as his father reappeared on the hiking path and dashed to the end of the dock. This was Alex's favorite part, he thought sarcastically, where his father stripped his shirt and shoes and jumped into the cool, clear water of the lake to swim laps. Alex watched for a minute, his irritation growing. The irony was that their culture was dependent on water. It was still a culture dependent on resources they did not have.

Alex noticed the train's distant approach. When it passed close to the open fire, he filled his messenger bag with a book on binary, his sketchpad, plus a copy of Orwell's *1984*. He adroitly swung off the roof and down a drainpipe.

As the train reached the platform and its doors opened, Alex was there to slip inside.

A camera followed his movements.

Chapter 10

Alex exited the train a couple miles from his house. He walked to the parking garage entrance of a strip mall grocery store. The garage was littered with abandoned cars.

The grocery was one of the last privately owned stores. It was a three-story structure, but only the first floor was in use. It was closed to the public now, but would open within the hour.

The open floor was about half full of goods, but most of the items could not be eaten. The inventory wasn't composed of new items. They were likely scavenged from abandoned homes or sold to the store by the original owners, a giant continuous garage sale.

All the food items were pushed into one tiny corner, a ploy to make people think there was still ample. Alex crept by the dishes, towels and cleaning products that lined the aisles. He hid from the cameras focused on the limited amount of cereal boxes, canned vegetables and packaged noodles.

The store had plenty of security. There were usually at least three guards who patrolled or watched the food corner from monitors. The store saved on its ration of electricity by keeping the lights dim when not open. Alex folded into a two-foot black void in the wall behind a security camera. He watched as one of the guards, a scarecrow of a man, put a bag of beans down the front of his pants.

Thievery wasn't as much of a problem as you would expect. There was a no tolerance policy. No effort was made to capture, bring to justice or imprison food thieves. They were simply killed on the spot. It took a lot of desperation to make the risk worth it.

Another security guard, one he didn't know, rushed out of the office. This guard's expression was humorless. Scarecrow saw the humorless guard note the suggestive bulge in Scarecrow's trousers. Scarecrow turned to make a pathetic run. Humorless raised his knife and plunged it into Scarecrow's back. Humorless grabbed Scarecrow by the foot and dragged him out of the store, leaving a trail of red as they went. How long had these two worked together? Alex wondered.

Alex waited until the store was empty before he unfolded his legs. He pulled a tattered Halloween mask from his bag and rested it on top of his head. His mom was pretty close to joining the zombies. He needed protein for her. He glanced back and forth between a small bag of nuts in a dim corner and a whole chicken set on a pedestal of light. He wanted the chicken, but he had to leave the camera's blind spot to get it. The nuts wouldn't last a day. He could make a stew with the chicken. It might last for a week. He pulled the mask over his face.

Alex knew Humorless was busy with Scarecrow. Alex made a grab for the chicken, tucked it into his messenger bag as he slid between two carts loaded with linens. He ran, low, in the faint light, favoring the camera's blind spots. He filled the messenger bag with potatoes and carrots. Even when he heard the third guard coming, he dashed into the center of the room and grabbed a couple chocolate bars.

He was fast, agile, as he dashed down a stopped escalator that led to the parking garage. He could hear the heavy steps of the third guard running behind him. An alarm sounded as Humorless joined the third guard in the chase. By his ear, he heard a whizzing sound the wires of a stun gun. Alex didn't dare look behind him. He doubled his pace until his lungs burned.

In the garage, he flipped himself over one abandoned car then crawled under three more until he reached a blue Honda hybrid. He used a key secured to his wrist with an elastic band to open the trunk of the car. He heaved himself into the back of the trunk, pulled a blanket over his head and slid a plastic laundry basket in front of him. He listened to the running and commotion outside the car. His breathing was thick and heavy in the dark. He grappled to regulate his rasping gasps.

"Where'd he go?" Humorless asked.

"I'm getting sick of this," the other answered. "I want my guns back."

"You never could shoot someone for shoplifting. At least now you can splat their brains with a baton or slit their throat with a knife."

Splat their brains. This guy was demented. Alex quaked in the trunk of the car more fearful than he'd been in a long time. He knew that if he were caught, his chances of escape from this confined space were slim. He listened to nothing intently for a long while.

When it was quiet and Alex felt safe, he fell into a light and anxious sleep.

Chapter 11

Early dawn, Alex hit the emergency release and slithered from the trunk of the car. The car had moved, as he knew it would, into his neighbor's driveway.

Alex circled to a back window and tapped. When the window lifted, he passed the key on the elastic band and the candy bars inside to Jared.

"Everything okay?" Jared asked.

"Sure," Alex answered in a hushed tone reserved for people who share secrets. "I'm going to make stew. Come over later."

Jared handed back one of the bars of chocolate. He nodded as he slid beneath the window and returned to bed.

He walked home. He went around to the front of his house and ran smack into the third security guard, Mr. Rydell.

"Hello Mr. Rydell." Alex waved.

"Morning Alex. You're up early. How's your mom feeling?"

"I think she'll be a little better soon."

Alex knew that today he was lucky, but his luck wouldn't last for much longer. He needed a better, more permanent solution.

Alex sat on the front porch stoop and lifted the Nomad given to him by his father. He viewed its small image, resolved to make the call he'd been putting off for months.

"Dad."

Frank came on the line. "Alex?

"I think you should come home."

Alex had called his father once before when Alex was about ten. He got the same answer this time as then.

"You know I can't."

Then as now, Alex waited for his father to ask what was wrong, to offer his help, but he didn't. Alex remembered that earlier conversation.

"The gates are locked," Frank had said. "It's complicated, but I'll see what I can do."

But he never did. So Alex fed his mother by stealing from a

grocery store that would soon close down and even that would no longer be an option.

In its place, the Wagner Group had built feeding stations, heavily armed kiosks where food was disbursed one person at a time, making a never-ending bread line.

Alex pulled a penknife from his pocket and used it to slice out the Nomad's embedded device under the skin of his hand. He set the bloody chip on the ground and stomped on it. He waited for a minute for the blood to begin to clot and then he wiped the blood from his hand on his pants leg.

Alex stared at Jeb Hauge's house across the street. It had burned to char and ash. The street was full of potholes with a rusty wreck of a car in front of the Hauge house. A clothesline was strung from the car to a nearby camera pole. This is where Jeb Hauge lived now.

At Alex's house, the landscaping had all turned to sand. The fifty-foot oak tree in the front yard had split, half falling onto the house, making parts unusable. Still, the door to the house was painted a slowly fading red and old cans had been converted to flowerpots that sported mint, dill and basil.

The cactus in the front yard was half shriveled. Yellow flowers struggled to faithfully bloom. Dying paddles littered the ground under it.

Alex grabbed an empty can that had once held refried black beans. He scooped a handful of sandy dirt into the bottom of the can and broke off one trailing stem of the cactus with three good buds on it. Careful of the painful, little barbs, he buried the stem into the sand.

Alex bounced up the slanted tree onto the roof of the house. He unlocked a padlock and opened a makeshift door. He flipped inside.

Alex landed in Etta's room. One wall was boarded over with stained two-by-four teak planks that covered the hole left by the fallen tree. Alex turned on an old box fan that blew hot air directly onto Etta. Alex had to trade his bike and a mint plant for the fan, but it was worth it.

Etta slept on a mattress on the floor where it was slightly cooler. She was thin and weak. Her bony fingers clenched a green sheet crusted with vomit. She woke and retched into a nearby bucket.

"Mom, you alright?" Alex asked. He set the buds on the floor beside her.

"Oh." She smiled. Her glassy eyes focused on him. "Morning Sweetie."

"Did you sleep?"

"Some. My back is aching a bit."

"How's the swelling in your feet and ankles?"

"Who's the doctor here?"

Alex lay down next to his mother. They played this game every day now, both not saying the many things that truly needed to be said.

"I dreamed of Lola again. She's waiting for me now."

His mother had a twin sister, Lola, who was a relief worker fighting starvation in North Africa after J-flu hit. They shut down travel and she was never able to make her way home.

Mom waited for her for many years. She tried to get word to her, but never heard back. Mom thought she knew the exact moment that Lola died. She felt it in her heart and in her soul. After that day, Mom no longer waited for Lola to return home. She made an alter for Lola on the console table under the family picture. She put framed photos and favorite things and she mourned for her lost sister.

"Shouldn't you be on your way to school?" Etta mustered her best mom-tone.

"You need to eat something."

"Go on. I'm okay. I'm not hungry."

The fan suddenly went off. The air hung heavy and still.

"Not again." Alex was annoyed. "The electricity is out."

"Have we reached our power ration already?"

"No." Alex answered. "It can't be that."

"I'll call Network Services and get a replacement object. You go to school."

Alex kissed her sweaty forehead. "No," he said. "I think I'll stay home with you today."

"Don't fuss. Go to school."

Alex knew he was defeated. "I'll call Network Services. And I'll make you a little toast and tea before I go."

Etta's eyes rolled in her head and she lost focus for a minute.

"I went to the store and got some chicken," Alex said. "I'll start a stew for lunch. I'll put it on the stove very low and be back in a couple hours to give it a stir. With the herbs you grow, it will be tasty. I can't wait."

He moved into a living room that had seen better days. He kept it clean for his Mom, but other than the few most needed pieces of furniture, the room was empty.

He looked at his hand. He would have a scar on it where he had dug out the Nomad biometrics. He had a beta version of the original Nomad model, one that didn't have all the intrusive security features. He went to his room and picked up the simple, handheld device from its charger. He pointed the Nomad at a blank wall. It shot up a 2D screen. No 3D on this model.

"Network Services," he said. He knew that no one at the other end could detect any difference between his old phone and any other network device, the biggest variation being that he could turn his off, hide if need be.

"Network Services. Detective Roget." She appeared on screen. She sat in a room crowded with computer equipment. A 2D display on a fifty-foot LCD screen filled a wall behind her. Alex tried unsuccessfully to focus on it, but he couldn't see what was there. She glanced at his face and sat up straighter. Alex wondered if she recognized him.

Anne had the same long wavy hair as his mother, except that Anne's hair was walnut brown, not the color of a tarnished penny that his Mom's was. Anne's amber brown eyes shined like she knew something you didn't know. She smiled reassuringly.

"I need a replacement object from the Repository," Alex said.

"What's the problem?" asked Anne, her face calm, neutral.

"Electricity. Power's off. We don't have any." Alex felt annoyed and wanted to take it out on Anne, but then he recognized her. Vixen.

Anne peeked at her computer. She checked their account. "That's a lot of kilowatt hours you have available," she said.

"We're very frugal," Alex offered.

Now, he knew, she was doing other troubleshooting.

"I do see some wonky here in your sector."

"Is that a technical term – wonky."

"Most people don't care to know more."

Alex watched Anne's fingers as she called up a long list of icons and selected the one for utilities, subfile: electricity, subfile: Sector 7. She did a copy and paste. On screen, Alex could see the message "Replacing Object 7418457."

Anne asked, "That working for you?" She looked at his identification. "Alexander."

"Alex. Only my mother calls me Alexander and only when she's mad."

Did he just see Anne scribble something on a slip of paper using a pencil? Yes. She tucked it into her pocket.

"What was your name again?" Alex asked.

"Detective Anne Roget."

Alex looked into Etta's bedroom. He heard a white noise as the fan came back on. Etta leaned back into the cooling breeze and relaxed. She closed her eyes and he saw her begin to drift off to sleep.

"Yes, Detective. The power is on. Thanks."

Since its beginning, the Famine had claimed many people, people with skills. The Repository kept a copy of all the critical computer programs. When something went wrong, Network Services personnel were trained to copy the original object from the library and replace the corrupt one. They couldn't fix it. They didn't know how. At this point, almost nobody could.

He wanted to give her something in return for her kindness to the dead. "You know you need to figure out the original code," Alex warned.

Anne said nothing, although her face said that she agreed with him.

He signed off and went into the kitchen. Before he made the toast for breakfast, he cut the chicken into cubes and put it into a cast iron pot with potatoes, carrots, water and a few herbs from the garden. He covered the pot and turned on the stove so that there was barely a flame. He'd come back at lunch and force her to eat some.

When Alex brought Etta the toast, he set a mobile device beside her with his new phone number preloaded into it.

"Call me if you need me. Okay?"

Etta nodded.

"Promise."

"Promise," Etta said. "Will you do something for me?"

"No," Alex responded. He kissed her cheek.

"What? You don't even know what I'm going to ask?"

"I'm not calling him." Alex walked out the door. He thought it best never to mention that he had already tried.

"Wear your sunsuit," Etta called after him in a thin voice.

"I'll be fine," he said as he put on his reflective cap. He slammed the living room door after him. "I'll be back soon."

Chapter 12

Etta lay on the mattress in her bedroom, her hand rested on the bucket. She couldn't focus her thoughts. One minute, she'd be sitting on the quad at college, two goofy guys walking up to her, both young, slim and vital. The next minute, she'd be on the elementary school playground, arms circled around her sister Lola as they danced in a downpour of rain. Then, she'd be in the nursery, putting down Alex for the first time.

Her Nomad beeped. She dreamed of a beach, lying in the hot sun. A drop of perspiration dripped down her nose. Her phone signaled again. She roused herself to consciousness. The heat was real. The drop of sweat was real.

"Hello." Her voice croaked and sounded weak even to her.

Sheala O'Dell, stern teacher in her sixties with bottle orange hair and intelligent, fiery eyes, appeared. She was agitated.

"Dr. Harvey. Is Alex coming to school?"

Sheala ran a one-room schoolhouse with about fifty students, many of which attended via camera connects.

"He may be a little late..."

Sheala moved closer to the camera, a severe look in her eyes. "He's not late. This will be his third absence this week."

"He knows how important his education is too me. He needs to learn to survive. Why would he..."

"I have a waiting list. I'm going to have to expel him."

"Expel?" Etta asked. "Not suspend? Please, don't do this?"

"He rarely comes to class. If you want your son to graduate high school, you and his father must come see me. We must discuss this situation."

"His father?" Etta exclaimed as Alex's teacher cut the connection.

Chapter 13

Alex mixed with the college crowd, half of whom were wearing protective gear and half not. He moved across a rambling lawn toward the main building. The building, a French-style castle with turrets of stone that were capped by a red tile roof, looked like decayed Ivy League.

On a pole facing the door of the building was a camera. It scanned the grounds and the entrance. Alex avoided its sweep as he skulked through the heavy wood door. He ambled down a long hall bordered by doors, light pouring from those entries that were open. The hall was poorly lit and near empty.

He entered an office door. Shelves filled with volumes of books lined the walls. In front of the ledges, stacks of books sat ready to tumble over. They covered all the available surface space, with the exception of a table that held several different models of computers from all different stages of development across time.

Alex traveled through the corridor of books to a small sitting area. No books here. Instead the shelves held movies in DVD cases that required an old computer to watch. The walls also sported an assortment of pictures: the horses from Chauvet Cave, fractals, the aura borealis over Iceland and Bryce Canyon in Utah. No matter how many times he walked by them, Alex couldn't help but be awed by the pictures.

An overstuffed easy chair in a battered geometric pattern was angled toward a tall window. Alex listened. He heard deep, labored breathing that seemed to have an echo. He glanced at a computer on a table. Darth Vader fought with Luke Skywalker on the Death Star.

Alex circled to the front of the easy chair. Ved, looking as archaic as his books, sat hooked to a respirator, raggedly breathing in and out, just like Darth Vader. Alex had asked Ved's about his biography. Ved had an impressive career as an inventor and teacher that he'd self-sabotaged when he wouldn't sell out to the Wagner Company. Now, with his lung issues, teaching two classes a semester at a local university wore him out.

Alex also asked Ved about the reports of his death. Ved looked haunted, chased by his ghosts and refused to talk about it. Silently, Alex had agreed that this part of his past was off limits.

Ved had a tattoo on one arm with an image that was hard to discern given the slackness of the skin on his arms, but Alex could see the number 22 in it, likely for the twenty-two scientists Ved worked with who died during the pandemic.

Alex moved a cracked brown leather jacket in order to sit in an opposing chair.

"There was a time when technology was so abundant that everyone had multiple devices." Ved had said this before. "Nobody left home without a smart phone or a tablet or a laptop or all of them. Attached at the hip," he said, "whooshing and pinging everywhere. People believed that there would always be more, new, better devices. Technology only progressed – then."

There were plenty of people around who remembered the many devices about which Ved reminisced.

"I wasn't 'all that'." He did finger quotes. "I was hardly a blip on the radar. Lots of people could program. Many more people could use. Applications were free on the Internet until big-dollar businesses created fences around their apps and began to charge for use." Ved's face was a complex mix of anger and wonder.

"And now you're a genius."

"For inventing a phone," he laughed.

Ved made light today, but there had been other days where he talked about the day his wife had been attacked and killed by murderers who wanted her hard drive—wanted her research. Alex knew Ved had a pale tattoo over his heart for his wife.

Alex touched the old man's hand, but said nothing.

Ved liked movies as much as books. He said that both books and movie disks had gone the same way as the food, only much sooner. With digital books, bookstores had become smaller and smaller, with all the items pushed deeper into the corner until the stores were no longer viable and had to shut down. Stores that sold movies went the same way. And now, the viewer could only obtain the movies and digital books that the Repository allowed.

Ved especially preferred a genre called science fiction and fantasy. Many of his favorite books and movies had disappeared from the Repository in recent years. Those were the ones about revolution. But Ved had saved them on otherwise unusable stand-alone equipment, old equipment—unregistered and not connected to any network. Ved studied revolution as if he was looking for hints, clues to how it was done.

Ved especially liked *Star Wars*. He remembered the long lines to get in. He talked about how this movie paved the way for lots of more realistic space tales and how he loved them all.

Star Wars was a story about a young man who put the good of the many over the needs of the one. The youth trained with a core of elite soldiers. Ved hadn't been interested in Alex, at first, until he noticed Alex's aptitude for electronics. Ved started training Alex to read and write computer code. He called Alex his elite soldier.

Alex thought the puppets were creepy and the robots were whiny, but liked the Star Wars scene where Luke battles his father. He suspected part of the reason Ved showed him this movie was its theme – Luke redeeming his totally evil father. Ved believed that fathers loved their sons. He believed that Alex's father, if motivated enough, would make the right choice, whatever the cost—just like Darth Vader.

Alex loved Ved like a father and he didn't need any other. He thought that they were much alike. Both of them were wrong collectors. Ved had accumulated a considerable list of wrongs against him, all of which Alex felt worthy of retribution. Alex's list was shorter. He hated the man who biologically gave him life.

Ved held an old computer on his lap. The monitor showed a camera that scanned the campus outside.

"You got hooked into police surveillance?" Alex asked.

Ved nodded. "I've been watching what they watch and you know what they watch? It's you. Some cop knows, just like I do, that you have a natural talent for subversion."

Alex pulled a desk chair up to the window. "The electricity went out again this morning. Guess who answered the phone?"

"And who was that?"

"Vixon."

With a burst of energy, Ved said, "Ha. What did I tell you?" He fell into a fit of coughing and wheezing.

"Take it easy. There's still a lot more you need to teach me, Yoda."

"Smart ass, you are."

Alex pulled the laptop to him. "Show me again, oh wise one, how you cracked the code."

Chapter 14

Alex got home at noon. He felt physically ill when he saw Charlie sitting in his kitchen eating the stew Alex had prepared for his mother. Charlie Broadnack was rotund. Sitting on their kitchen stool, his rolls of fat folded over making him look like a snowman – three round balls. Alex was moving to take the bowl out of Charlie's hand when Mom spoke up.

"Say hello to Charlie, Alex. I invited him to lunch."

Alex stopped for her sake, but he was still livid.

"How was school this morning?" Mom asked.

"Fine," Alex said. "I learned a lot."

Mom looked at him askance. Alex wasn't sure what the look meant.

Alex slammed open the cabinet looking for something else for Mom to eat.

Mom lay on the living room sofa. Charlie moved next to her and sat on the cushion at one end. He rubbed her feet. Alex didn't like that either.

Mom had made an effort for Charlie. She had gotten out of bed, taken a shower and put on clean clothes. Maybe that was a touch of blush on her cheeks or maybe she had overexerted herself. Alex couldn't be sure.

Alex looked toward the island between the kitchen and living room. A stuffed bag sat on the counter. He went over and peeked inside. Peaches, green beans and a half dozen cans of soup. He opened a can of vegetable soup and heated it.

"Your dad does a good job," Charlie stood and moved closer to Alex. "Those peaches are big. Shall I put some in your backpack? I was thinking that you could take them to the park tonight. Find a pretty girl and show her a good time."

Charlie picked up Alex's messenger bag and transferred some of the peaches inside. That enraged Alex, this invasion of his personal property. He jerked the bag away from Charlie. One of the peaches rolled off the kitchen counter and hit the floor.

"Something going on in a park?" Alex responded, cold as ice. Alex ducked down and picked up the peach. He tossed it back to Charlie.

That chicken was supposed to last for a week, Alex thought as he poured the thin canned soup into a cup. He brought it to his mother and held the cup to her lips.

Alex knew he should be grateful for the food that Charlie brought. Instead, he wanted to pop Charlie one in the nose. He should say thank you for his mother's sake, but he just couldn't. They were beholden to Charlie for the scraps he supplied. Maybe that was why Mom got out of bed and dressed up, she felt indebted too.

Alex went into his Mom's bedroom and pulled the soiled sheets off the bed. He would wash those later. He opened a plastic bin, pulled out clean sheets and made the bed. Charlie hadn't given up his topic when Alex returned to the living room.

"I've heard about the bartering that goes on," Charlie said, "in a park." It was more of a question than a statement.

Alex felt a little panicky, but tried not to show it. He was being pumped for information.

Alex had learned from Ved how to compress and plant a hidden file into an image. He'd send out a random picture of something cute or funny like babies or cats with the embedded file in it. It used to be an announcement for when the farmer's market was scheduled, but it had grown to include declarations of rights and other calls for equality and equity.

"The park. That sounds cool," Alex said. "Where is it?"

"I thought you would know."

"Why would I?"

When Alex was ten, he had called and Charlie had come when his dad had not. Within a month, Charlie had started stopping by with bits of food, just enough to keep a hamster alive. They had taken his generosity for the last nine years. He had brought enough food to taunt, but not enough to save his mother.

The damage to Etta's organs was permanent. Her body had responded to starvation by using her already damaged kidney tissue to make energy. She had become an unwilling anorexic.

"Mom, you look tired." Her skin was a yellow color too, but he didn't mention that. "Do you want to go back to bed? Take a little nap?" Alex asked. She hardly touched the broth.

Charlie answered for her. "We're going to set up the checker board. I'm going to let your Mom beat my ass."

"Language is meant to be precise," Etta said as she always did when someone cursed.

"He's a big boy," Charlie responded. "He knows exactly what I mean."

Alex pulled Charlie to one side. "Look at her. She needs to go back to bed. You're taxing her too much." Alex walked Charlie to the door. "Say goodbye to my mom," I called into the room. "Charlie has to go back to work. He'll see you another time."

Alex pushed Charlie out the door.

He headed for his room. He had barely set down his messenger bag when he heard a tap at the window. He slid back the curtains. Jared was there.

"He's here?" Jared asked.

"Peaches, big ones."

Jared made a sound, yummy and satisfied. "Enough?"

Alex opened the messenger bag and handed a large juicy piece of fruit to Jared. "There's always enough for you."

Jared smiled.

"Park later?" Alex asked.

Jared nodded.

"But I think we should change the time, make it a few hours earlier. I'll send out a bat signal."

Chapter 15

When Alex was younger, the cooling center, formerly the Austin Historic Downtown Post Office, had been the best place to hang out. The adults stayed quiet and occupied. They chatted as they sewed or quilted. The Post Office had long since shut down, but sometimes at the cooling center you could get a message or a letter from a loved one. The letters always told of the travails of living elsewhere. In the cooling center, they clicked out potholders and blankets as fast as they could while they applauded themselves for having this place to which they could escape.

In the early days of the drought, demand for electricity had been much higher than availability. Originally, the question was 'how can we provide a constant source of power to everyone?' Even though they had jacked up rates by an amount that should have been beyond the ability of most people to pay, the demand for power had continued to outstrip its supply. Eventually, carefully rationed power had been restored to people's homes on the outside. The question then became 'how much power can be provided, regardless of how many people might want or need it?'

Jared had made a potted plant garden at home. Many people did this, planting herbs and vegetables under their windows in anything that would hold dirt. Jared also grew a medicinal herb that his law and order father seemed to overlook.

That's why the older kids let Alex and Jared hang out with them at the cooling center. They crammed into a corner, backs against a wall, knees up and passed a homemade pipe from hand to hand as if no one saw.

Alex didn't care so much about the reefer. What he liked was fifteen-year-old Sonia. Her lustrous, strawberry-blonde hair hung straight and smooth like satin flowing over her shoulder and down her back. Alex wanted so much just to touch it. It had to be soft, like a kitten's coat.

Sonia came to the cooling center with her grandfather. Once she'd get him set up with his book, she'd drift over to talk to her friend Trix. Trix cared about the reefer.

One day, Sonia glanced over her shoulder toward him and Alex could hear nothing but the pounding in his ears. She looked like she stepped out of that Vermeer's painting of the Girl with Pearl Earring except she had on Daisy Duke shorts, a tiny tank top with an old man's button-down hanging loose over it. Thank you Daisy Duke, whoever you are.

"Want to meet my grandfather?" Sonia asked him. Jared and Trix were testing out French kissing. He wanted to do that. He didn't want to meet an old man, but what could he do? "Sure," Alex said.

Alex kept a blasé face, but this ancient elder with his wheezy breath scared him. His shroud of black clothes also didn't help.

"Anything about this cooling center strike you as odd?" the old man asked ignoring any formalities like saying hello. His face was somewhat hidden by a hoodie.

"It's the only decent place left in town."

"Exactly. Think boy think. Why is that?"

It didn't appear to be a question to which this old man needed an immediate answer, but it did start Alex pondering. Why, when each household was only allowed ten kilowatts of electricity and twenty gallons of water per household per day, was this cooling center blasting energy?

Alex thought about Jared's father's grocery store. It thrived as long as it had the appearance of giving people what they wanted, not the reality. If you gave people a little something, it was easier to take away the things they really needed. Alex's eyes searched the walls and ceiling. That's when he spotted it. A camera. He knew they were being watched. He realized that this cooling center was a way of monitoring and controlling them.

"Fuck." Alex flinched. "Sorry. I know language should be more precise."

Sonia's old grandfather struggled up from his chair and hobbled over to Alex.

"What," he asked, "are you willing to give up for food, for electricity? Are you willing to give up your freedom?

Yes, Alex thought, but said nothing. "What do you want?" Alex asked the old man.

"I want people to go beyond fighting only for themselves and take up arms to fight together."

The next trip to the cooling center was accented by more provocative questions and then the old man gave Alex a slip of paper.

"I can teach you how to hack into the home panel grid, he said. Come to see me and I will," he said.

The next day, Alex went to a dank office, full of musty books and the smell of old man. Sonia sat at a library table and chewed on the tips of her hair as she read a book. A lamp made of colored glass panels cast a warm light on her face and hands. She raised her eyes to him from time to time with that glow in them as well and he grew so flustered he could not think.

But soon her grandfather's words pierced his haze. He listened when the geriatric talked. And read when the old man gave him a couple of books: <u>The History of Global Revolution</u> and <u>The Life and Times of Gandhi</u>.

"Alex," he said. "We're going to start a coup."

That's how old-man Ved, Sonia's grandfather, became Alex's Yoda.

Chapter 16

Frank shut his drawing pad and set the book on his living room sofa. His pencil rolled off the cushion and fell to a floor covered in crushed papers. He didn't bother to retrieve it.

The bay window's heavy, wooden blinds were open. Bright afternoon light poured into Frank's eyes like lasers. With effort, Frank rose up from the couch, shut the blinds and then lifted one slat to peer outside. Nothing much going on.

Frank hard-boiled an egg, sliced and inserted it between his last two pieces of stale bread. The carton for the eggs was now also empty. He wasn't really hungry, but he hadn't eaten since yesterday. Maybe some coffee would perk him up.

He shook the container that held the coffee and noted that he was almost out. He opened a cabinet to reveal a half empty jar of Nutella. A couple roaches moved, but in no particular hurry to escape the sudden light.

Inside his mini refrigerator, he saw a jar of Wasabi paste, a jar with olives and two limes. Frank started a grocery list using his drawing pencils and a crumpled bit of paper he picked up from the floor.

"Screen One," Frank said. He'd do the groceries in a minute. He had all the time in the world. Nothing but time. Instead, he started a digital game of Spider Solitaire using three decks of cards.

When a shrill alarm went off on her Nomad, Etta forced herself to sit up in bed. She had showered and dressed earlier in the day. She intended to rise and go to her 3:30 p.m. meeting with Alex's teacher, but she soon realized that she didn't have the energy. She lacked the lifeforce. She couldn't do it. The school was only four blocks down the street, but she didn't think she could make it. She had to call Franklin who had developed this glowering dissonance that may only be in her mind, but it felt real to her. It made it difficult for her to talk to him.

Franklin had a complicated relationship with aloneness. He had felt unwanted as a small child. He'd lived in an emergency shelter for orphaned or abandoned children his first six years. Other boys came and went to new homes, but because he had a heart defect, he wasn't picked. His heart had been repaired and he was taken to foster by the Hogar family over the next ten years, but the feeling seemed to have stuck. He wasn't wanted because his heart was flawed.

He still believed that his heart was damaged, broken. He lived in a virtual cave of his own making. He was stingy with words and gestures.

Etta thought that learning to love was a skill, a life lesson that had to be taught by a person. She knew that Franklin hadn't learned when he was young. She had hoped she could be that person for him.

She had a brief moment before she married him. She was in the library with her psychology books in front of her and looked up his personality traits in a diagnostic manual. She found the autistic spectrum. His withdrawal wasn't severe. He didn't have tics or compulsions. He could connect with people without sweating or panic if he wished. He made eye contact — unless he chose not to. He may be autistic, but not by much. Aloneness was his choice.

She believed that Franklin created his own self-fulfilling prophecy. He was afraid of pain and the disappointment people often brought, so was just unavailable to them. She tried her best, but eventually it seemed he included her and Alex among the disappointing. This was especially true since Franklin entered the dome, that absolute barrier.

These were all things she'd learned to cope with in their marriage, but they weren't the reason they broke up. They were the reason they didn't communicate better now.

She flicked the Nomad and projected a screen against the wall. Franklin didn't answer, so she left a message.

From the desk, Frank picked up his shopping list. He plopped back down on the sofa, his unkempt hair falling into his eyes. He licked his palm, wrist to fingertip, and pressed his hair to his head.

"Computer," he said. He looked at the hopelessly lost game of Spider Solitaire on the wall. "Screen one. Switch to Wagner Company." His failed game disappeared and a series of cold, sterile images appeared that introduced the Wagner Company. The computer asked for his employee ID number in a digitized and toneless voice.

"Franklin Harvey, 2976."

Frank touched the device in the flesh of his fingers between thumb and index. It read his heart rate and knew his voice.

"Etta Harvey calling," his Nomad informed him. A still image of her face popped up.

"Really?" The computer was smart enough to ignore such rhetorical comments.

"Would you like to connect to Etta Harvey?"

"No. No. Not yet."

Frank felt restless, but he didn't have the energy to talk to Etta. He paced his tiny living room. He had done his run at his usual time in the morning, but he felt so lethargic he decided that he'd take another short jog now – before he made the call. He added a tee shirt and running shoes to his shorts and headed out the door.

He stood under the overhang of his swimming deck. He looked down the pier at the neat row of houseboats dotting the lake on each side. His breathing had picked up even though he had not yet started his run.

He allowed himself a glance toward the dome's gate. The zombies were out there, dozens of them. The transparent surface of the dome gave them a wavy, blurred appearance, skeletal demons from hell. Frank forced his eyes away from the gate.

He ran. He dashed down the pier toward the lake and then jumped from the pier to the hiking trail. He ran past the river and through the orchards. He ran like ghosts were chasing him.

A farmer pruned some small plants at the hydroponics farm. He stopped and waved to Frank. "Nice day," he called and Frank nodded like it was, like any day was.

Frank circled past the largest building inside the dome, the glass and steel structure with an ornate sign that announced that it was "The Wagner Company."

In the distance was the power station with its armed guards at the entrance. They watched him alertly as he stormed past, never giving him so much as a nod.

He tired as he hit the last leg of his run. He dashed to the end of the pier, stripped off his shirt and shoes and jumped into the lake. Having exorcised his demons sufficiently, he pulled himself out of the water by a ladder on the piling of the pier and headed home.

Frank showered, dressed and tamed his hair. He sat on the sofa and called for two more 2D screens next to the first screen showing his Wagner Company worksite. He switched his focus back and forth between the three screens displayed on his long wall.

"Screen one. Check wholesale."

Stores of food items and the amounts available scrolled down the screen. "Send sixty-five percent of available peaches to the online store for dome inhabitants. Send thirty percent to Sector 7, 9 and 15 city stores outside. Distribute the thirty percent evenly." He watched the figures on screen refresh.

"Screen two. Show news." The second screen showed the fire raging outside the dome. "Firefighters estimate that the blaze is ninety percent contained at this point," a newscaster reported. "Need I say again that the burn ban is still in effect..."

Frank set the third screen to the weather channel. It showed a weather radar map that was pale green. There was no variation in color.

The forecaster said, "Today marks the twenty-fourth anniversary of the start of the drought. As usual, there is no chance of rain in the foreseeable future."

Frank had been seventeen that year. From six to eighteen, he'd lived with the Hogars. They had a full house of their own kids. He felt second-rate to them, and so he would take his sorta brother Denny's iPad and walk in the woods behind the Hogar's house. He liked to read or game. He liked being on his own in the quiet and stillness of nature.

Frank had read a book about civilizations that survive the test of time. The book indicated one thing they all had in common was the willingness to live within the limits of their own natural resources. When they didn't, the world fell out of balance and fought back. He had believed that then. Still did.

The local radar map switched to a national one — the same national map they always showed. No one was forecasting to them from other states.

"And at the national level, what a night. Seven tornadoes in the mid to northeast....

Frank said. "Screen one. Send five percent of peaches from District 7 to the FFEA account. Copy to Charles Broadnack. Show green beans."

Frank switched his attention to screen two.

"Spraying for new infestations of spiders, ants and roaches will begin later this week. Remember to store food only in sealed containers or in your refrigerator."

Frank's anxiety was rising again. "Screen two off. Screen three off." Frank sat in silence for a minute. "Okay. Call Etta."

Frank awakened Etta from a little nap she clearly hadn't meant to take. Her face was startling: yellow-pale, gaunt and pained. He thought about it. He hadn't talked to Etta in person in months. She emailed regularly with reports of Alex, but no face contact.

"What's wrong?" Frank asked with true concern in his voice.

Etta responded. "Alex is in trouble at school. His teacher plans to expel him."

"What'd he do?"

"I don't know. I need you to take care of it. One of us must appear today at three-thirty and I'm feeling a little under the weather."

"Are you okay? You look awful."

"I'm fine," she said, but he wasn't sure he believed her.

In theory, anyone could get a pass from Wagner to have dome security let him inside or outside of the dome. In fact, no one from the outside had ever been allowed in unless they worked for the Wagner Company. But Frank assumed that getting out temporarily might not be as hard. He didn't know for certain because he'd never tried it. He didn't know anyone who had. The question was if you went out, could you get back in? Just the idea of requesting a pass brought beads of sweat to Frank's forehead. He rubbed his palms on the fabric of the sofa.

"I'll call his teacher and reschedule," Frank said.

"It's time for you to reconnect with your son," Etta said. "Be a better father."

"Etta," he said.

He saw Etta grab a bucket before she blocked his view. He took her long silence as an accusation. He launched his defense when she came back online.

"I contact Alex every week. I can't help it if he won't respond."

"Listen to what I'm saying. I need you to take care of our son Alexander."

Frank didn't answer, but his expression was worried.

"You know," Etta continued, "this bubble you live in protects you from the good parts of life as well as the bad."

She hung up.

Chapter 17

Revolutions start small. This revolution began by moving the gathering spot from the Cooling Center to what once was an old Victorian estate that had long ago been converted to an upscale restaurant, but was now abandoned. The grounds were completely surrounded by fencing and there was no surveillance. The estate had fallen into disuse and disrepair, but it was still privately owned property, and therefore less subject to government or police scrutiny. And, it was still lovely in its own way with many old cypress and fruit trees hanging on to life on a ten-acre lawn now turning to dust. An occasional peafowl might be spotted on the trees' bare branches. Imaginatively, they called this secret garden "The Park." Alex stepped through a blind made of old branches and boards and smiled at the sight.

In the six months after meeting Sonia at the cooling center, they had become inseparable. It didn't matter what Sonia was doing, Alex wanted to be with her. She often joined him on his visits to see Ved at the college, sitting quietly in a corner teaching herself how to knit. She'd come to his house in the evenings and worked in his father's slowly dying garden, struggling to bring it back to life. And Sonia and his mom became fast friends. Sonia sat by Mom's bedside telling her stories of her life that were possibly meant for Alex to overhear.

It was Sonia's mother's idea to create a market. Isa was resourceful and creative. She knew how to make many things with her hands. From Isa's vast contacts, she and her friends quietly organized the mothers, grandmothers and even a few great grandmothers who wore loose, flowing skirts made of natural fabrics and had hair they never cut. They knew how to make candles, soaps and quilts. They grew organic plots in their backyard. Sometimes they kept chicken coops for fresh eggs. They also found woodworkers, tinkers and iron smiths. Back in before days, these people had organized community gardens, farmer's markets and street festivals. They were smart, capable and organized.

Once the electricity became more widely available, Sonia's father, Rory, advertised the markets. He had a television program that aired once a day, but otherwise the channel showed only weather radar. Having the information so widely publicized drew raiders and thieves, and so Ved set up a private network. He turned the whole project over to Alex who set up a secure schedule for trade days on the nomad. People came with a nice variety of goods and services to barter or sell and it worked peacefully.

Wagner thought of himself as an autocrat. He made it illegal for anyone but his company to sell food in bulk. Wagner ranted about bartering that excluded him, but so far he had not found The Park. Just in case, people were told never to bring more to barter than they could carry. The idea was that people could slip into safe houses in the neighborhood if there was a raid by Wagner's security forces — for this is who Alex blamed for all the attacks.

Alex split off from Jared who headed toward Trix. Alex made straight for Sonia.

Sonia's shiny hair was loose. She held its strawberry richness with her slim fingers and lifted it for a moment from the back of her neck. Alex flushed warm remembering its tickle on his chest, her breath warm on his bare skin as she hovered over him in his bed the night before.

Her mouth twitched ever so slightly as it had done last night when he had touched her cheek in the dim light. He had savored her face, memorizing each tiny expression. She had leaned down into a deep kiss, breathing her breath into him. Her lips had tasted of mint and honey.

Sonia pulled a small watermelon from her shopping bag. It reminded him of her smell, subtle and sweet. It was not the smell of a specific flower or fruit, but pure Sonia. It should be bottled as a perfume.

She spoke softly to a vendor who held candles. Softly, like she did when she had whispered to him, "I love you." Then she had looked into his eyes and he shut them. Why did he do that? His mother would have smothered her in kisses and said that he loved her too. Maybe he was more his father's son than he wanted to admit.

"That's all right," she'd said before she fell asleep in his arms, but he could tell that she was hurt and confused that he had not said that he loved her too.

Alex folded his fingers around her forearm and felt the goose bumps rise on her flesh. He took her into his arms and kissed her gently, but full on the mouth. It was by way of an apology. Sonia blushed, but she didn't pull away, and so he did it again. Like him, Sonia was shy about public displays of affection. Despite that, her hand trailed down his back and rested on his butt.

"Four candles," the vendor said with a lecherous grin. "That's my final offer."

Alex lifted the watermelon from Sonia's long fingers. "Look at this. It's a melon made of water, a watermelon, wet, and sweet. I can almost feel the juice running down my hands. It's worth at least..." he paused and Sonia held up five fingers, "...six candles," he said. "And some matches."

The vendor appraised Alex for a few seconds. "She said five. I'll give her five."

Alex nodded toward a small child, obviously the vendor's son. The son's eyes were filled with hope and expectation that he would soon be eating the melon. "Six."

The vendor followed Alex's nod to the boy. He was sunk. He added two candles to the four in his hand. "You drive a hard bargain."

Alex looked at the twin smiles of the boy and Sonia. "And everyone is happy at the end."

He bought Sonia a sun-made hibiscus mint ice tea and a bag of tealeaves with one of his peaches. He escorted Sonia to a webbed lawn chair where she sat, sipped her tea and chatted with Trix.

Alex looked with annoyance at the many chairs sitting in a neat little circle. Heavy chairs. The plan was to be easily mobile, to be able to move and hide. They were getting blasé and careless. He would have to set up a meeting.

An hour later, Alex shimmied up a post and sat at a makeshift bird's nest at the top. He fiddled with the workings of the light on top. Sonia's smile lit the whole park for him. He didn't need a light as long as he had her, but others weren't so fortunate.

Alex called down to Sonia in a loud whisper anyone near could hear. "I've been working on something new. A surprise for him."

"That's not the point. We're making our world better, not his world worse," Sonia said.

"So you say."

From his lofty vantage point, Alex spotted Wagner Company security forces gathering a couple blocks away. They were in four electric vans with blackened windows. Alex barely remembered vans. Everyone walked or took the light rail wherever they went. There was no fuel for anything else.

From his belt, he unclipped a mini air horn and set it off. It screeched a blaring warning to the people in the park. They would quickly gather everything that they could and make their way to one of several safe homes in the bordering neighborhood. At least that was the plan. In reality, they hesitated. They stayed too long.

"Let's go," Alex yelled. "Move."

From his perch, Alex saw the Wagner force move in behind riot shields. They wore tactical vests and ballistic helmets. They came in swinging heavy batons. It was all overkill. What did they expect? The park people weren't fighters. They didn't even talk badly about others.

It happened so fast. Jared and Trix were down before Alex had jumped off the light pole. Alex caught a glimpse of red hair, pushed along by a guard. Sonia was screaming for him as she fought against her captors. Alex swung widely from the pole, his legs knocking down the nearest invader. Alex kicked away a taser as he blocked the force of a guard swinging a baton. He ran in the direction he had last seen Sonia disappearing. He saw her being pushed by guards into a van. She thrashed against them until one of the guards socked her full fist in the face.

After that, Alex didn't see anything at all.

When he woke, he was in the safe house. The candle vendor and the tinker had carried him there. Jared and Trix were there. He looked around for Sonia with no luck.

"Where is she?" he asked Jared.

Jared shook his head. "I don't know."

Despite the throbbing in his head, Alex rolled up, stood and stumbled out the front door.

He sprinted the four blocks to the light rail station. He waited impatiently for the train. It felt like hours, but was in fact less than two minutes. He wanted to run all the way to the University, but he knew in his mind that the train would be faster.

He wasn't half way up the lawn toward the main building when he saw the black van parked at a side entrance. With a lot of fight for an old man without his respirator, Ved kicked and hollered as he was carried out.

Alex ran, but they were gone before he got close. He futilely chased the van.

He didn't wait for the train a second time. He ran toward the dome until his breath was ragged and his muscles cramped.

Alex positioned himself in his spot on the top of the train station. He waited.

He perked up when a vehicle, a smallish black van with the Wagner Company logo on its side, approached the gate. It stopped at the entrance and a squad of dark-clothed men exited the van.

They carried the limp body of a red-haired girl and an old man into the dome. Alex stood and trained a pair of field glasses on them as they dumped the sack of old man inside the gate.

Sonia and Ved were trapped inside the dome.

Chapter 18

Alex burst in the front door. "Mom." He set his canvas messenger bag on the kitchen counter. He glanced at the groceries on the counter he had from the bag that Charlie had left at lunchtime: peaches, green beans and some cans of soup.

"Mom. I'm gonna heat up some soup for dinner." He looked at a can of split pea soup. "And then we're going to pack a bag. I'm moving you," he wanted to say 'to someplace safer,' but how would he explain that. "I'm taking you to your hospital. I know you said 'no,' but I think we should. You need care and I need to…," what would he say – *save Sonia and Ved*?

He pulled out a pan and was halfway to the stove when he stopped. He listened to the silence in the house. It was total. Complete.

"Mom?"

His parents tried to never argue in front of Alex, but once he heard them going at it from the hall. That's what he thought about as he stood in the silent corridor waiting to build the nerve to go inside his mother's bedroom. He felt wary.

He tapped at the door. He sucked in air, but the room still felt like it didn't contain any oxygen. He didn't realize he had been holding his breath.

"Mom?" He gave the half-closed door a little push. He couldn't see her on the bed and he felt hopeful for a moment. He opened the door all the way.

She lay on the floor near her bed. Her arms and legs were bent in unnatural positions, like she had fallen where she landed. Her hair was matted with vomit and he smelled other secretions. She was still, silent and gray. He watched her, waiting for the rise and fall of her chest to resume, but it didn't.

Two feet away from her hand was the Nomad phone he had given to her that morning.

Alex felt himself coming out of a stupor. From the absence of sunlight at the window, he knew he'd been sitting on the floor for hours. He had pins and needles in his legs as he uncurled them. His eyes and throat burned from the crying. He glanced at the clock. He'd been keeping watch over her for about seven hours. He called for the death cart.

Alex changed the sheets on her bed as he had done a hundred times before. He picked her up gingerly in his arms and placed her carefully on the bed. He washed the vomit from her hair and brushed it from her forehead. As he changed her blouse, he spotted the ribbon around her neck.

They had talked a couple weeks ago. She had been trying to say goodbye, but he didn't want to hear it. First, she had said, no hospital. There was no point. She was the last doctor. She told him she wished to die at home.

As she lost weight, her wedding ring had slipped off her finger. Alex had found some ribbon and tied the ring around her neck. She had grabbed his hand. "When I'm gone," she had said, "I want you to take the ring and give it to the girl you love." She held it up for him to see. "It's an art deco design with three channel cut diamonds. "Precious. And valuable. Especially now."

Alex lifted her hair and pulled the ribbon over her head. He slipped the ring around his neck. He closed her eyes.

In a little while, two emergency medical techs carried a stretcher through his home. Alex gave the techs two peaches to ensure their best care for his mother.

Alex noticed the blinking of Etta's mobile on the floor. He picked it up. "You have one new message."

Alex stared at the device blankly. In a minute, his default response kicked in. He pushed the button.

"Playing first message." His teacher's voice floated toward him. "Dr. Harvey. I'm waiting for you or your husband. Did we have a miscommunication on the time?"

Alex deleted the message. He scanned through Etta's history. Her last outgoing call was to Frank Harvey. He viewed their conversation as the EMT's carried the stretcher with his mother's body out of their home.

Alex followed the EMT outside, closed the front door and locked it. He hurried to catch up. He walked beside the death wagon as if in a scene from out of the fourteenth century. Alex clutched Etta's Nomad in his hand.

When Alex returned to a silent and empty house, he went directly to his bedroom and powered up his old MacBook. He beat on the keyboard furiously. He pounded out his anger.

Chapter 19

Anne watched a 3-D image. The biodome decorated the distance as a few people exited the train station and walked down an otherwise desolate downtown street. Most wore head-to-toe metallic sunsuits to protect themselves from the sun's burning rays. They looked like astronauts from a hostile world.

Someone, hidden by his shiny covering, entered the police station, a four stories tall, old white building among other old white buildings near the city core. At one time, the police station had been the central library, but the library had been taken over when a location was needed for the Repository. Later, it just made sense to co-locate the police station with network services.

Pretty-boy Officer Zach Garland took off his sunsuit hood as he walked into the bullpen. Garland had a swagger and arrogance that got on Anne's last nerve, but he was also very bright and almost as competent on the computer as she. Anne led a small team who tried to relearn the original, unique, proprietary software for the Repository. Her team mostly worked from books and stand-alone computers. They had to be careful because the Repository code was full of traps.

Garland stopped and gawked over Anne's shoulder at the computer code displayed on the monitor on her desk.

The bullpen was in a large room crowded with computer equipment, but very few people. Some old-style monitors sat on desks and displayed 2D code or graphics. Other screens displayed on random walls that pumped 3D images of different parts of the city.

Garland passed through the 3D image of the train station as he walked toward his desk, piercing it like a ghost figure.

With great intensity, Anne studied code on an old-style Dell desktop. She rubbed her forehead. Behind her desk, a wedding photo of she and her deceased husband Nathan sat on a credenza. Above it was a virtual white board, more white than not. At the top was a blank square with a question mark. Below that Anne was working out a timeline.

"At it again?" Garland tilted his head toward the raw code on her screen. He craned his neck to investigate what she was doing.

Anne turned her monitor away from him. "It's our job."

"You ever experiment?"

"It's too risky to experiment with the code." Anne snapped at him. She exited the program she was reviewing. "You could hit a bug, release a virus and bring the whole Repository down."

The tone sounded for an incoming call. Pierce Wagner's angry blue eyes filled the screen. "I want you to follow a boy and tell me his comings and goings," he said.

"Pierce, I don't work for you any longer."

"Everyone who eats answers to me."

"Why? What's he done?"

"For one thing, I think he's stealing from my company."

Anne wondered what the other thing might be, the one Pierce wasn't telling her. "Who is it? What's his name?"

"Alex Harvey," Pierce responded.

Anne glanced at a scrap of paper where she had written in pencil the name "Alexander Harvey." *Call me Alex*, she remembered Alex saying. Pierce had gotten Alex's name from someone who knew him, maybe someone he trusted.

"You know him," Pierce accused.

"I don't know him. I see him sometimes on camera. That's all."

"And you've done nothing. It's almost like you're not trying, isn't it? I'd hate to find out that was true." He hung up before she could respond. Just as well. Anne had no clue what she might say next anyway.

Garland was still there, butting into her business. Garland used charm and a ready smile to hide a shiftiness she knew was just beneath the surface. Anne wondered, not for the first time, if he spied for Pierce on the side.

A network alarm sounded. It wasn't like any sound she had ever heard. It was insistent, loud. Anne jumped in her seat, looking concerned. A warning message popped up on all the screens in the room.

"What the hell?" Garland asked.

Anne's fingers flew across her keyboard and, in a minute, it was quiet. Anne and Garland exchanged panicked looks, but whatever it was seemed to be over.

Now she really had to wonder what Pierce knew that she did not.

Chapter 20

Inside his houseboat, Frank shot upright from the sofa. He was sweating even though all he wore was a pair of running shorts. He felt disturbed from a nightmare he'd just had, but couldn't quite remember. He sucked in a breath.

Frank imaged endless days in front of him all on his own, all alone. He stood and paced his small space back and forth for a nearly endless time, like a caged tiger. He felt isolated and a little crazy. He stared out his front window for a minute checking to see what activity lay just beyond his walls and then went back to pacing until his tiger stripes blurred.

Finally, he dropped to his knees in front of the sofa. He unclasped a Velcro panel on the underside, jammed his hand into the space and felt around. He smiled when he found what he was seeking. He pulled out a small canister with a facemask attached. It was labeled Fresh Air. He held the canister to his mouth and nose and took a long satisfying hit of pure oxygen. He buckled to the floor and took another hit.

He didn't have to go into the kitchen to see that the coffee can was still empty, sitting on the counter with a trail of small ants making off the last unused grounds.

Frank licked his palm and pressed down his hair. From his spot on the floor, he called out. "Computer on. Screen one. Grocery."

An online grocery store displayed row after row of pictures of fresh food. "Coffee," he said.

A message ran across the screen – "Eat this." Frank's computer flickered, made a couple odd noises and then went dead. Silent blackness. Frank shook his Nomad. Nothing.

Frank took another hit from the canister. "Coffee, I need coffee," he whimpered.

For an hour, Frank sat hunched over with his hands between his knees. He stared at his reflection in the windows. He looked small and helpless. Frank had a bad feeling. The longer his computer stayed down, the more his panic grew. Everything would be fine, if only he could make himself believe it.

He got up to pace. He went to the window and lifted a blind. Between the open slats on Cy's front window, Frank could see Cy twitching like a rabbit as he watched 3D porn.

"Computer on."

Frank ran his thumb over a security port on his left hand, but still got nothing. "Network Services," he tried to no avail. His computer was his lifeline to the world. The computer was his food, his work, and his connection to his family. It was everything. He needed a replacement object.

Frank went to his neighbor's houseboat and knocked on Cy's door. Cy opened a small, grated window in the front door.

"Who is it?" Cy asked although he could plainly see.

"Hi. I'm Frank Harvey. I live next door."

Cy offered no greeting. He studied Frank, his eyes darting around, his upper lip quivering.

"I'm down," Frank continued. "I need to contact Network Services. May I please use your computer?"

"I don't let strangers into my home."

"I've lived next door to you for a decade."

Cy didn't respond.

"I know you know who I am. I've seen you watching me."

"What're you saying? Are you saying that I peep?"

"Look. I just want to make a call."

"Come around to the side."

Frank walked to the bay window that he could see from his own houseboat. Cy pulled up the blinds and lifted the window. Cy used his Nomad to display a screen on a far wall. The opening of the window was too high for Frank to see comfortably from the pier.

"This is absurd."

"Network Services," Cy told the computer. An operator answered. The digital voice was reassuring and warm.

"I need to make a trouble report. My computer is down," Frank said.

"Please scan."

"I told you. I'm down. I'm at my neighbor's." Cy slid a chair up to the window and sat down. He chuckled softly.

Please state your name.

"Franklin Harvey."

Please state your name.

Cy responded loudly, "Franklin Harvey."

"Voice print is not a match."

Frank stared down Cy until he became uncomfortable enough to get up and walk a few steps away.

"Franklin Harvey," Frank repeated.

"I'll connect you."

The screen image went to Cy's screen saver, a series of beautiful, unobtainable women. Frank watched Cy move around in his kitchen. Cy was pretending to do something at his stove as he listened in.

Anne's image appeared on the wall. She was pretty, so Cy moved a couple steps closer to her image and switched her to 3D.

"Network Services. Detective Roget."

"Are you a person?" Frank asked.

Anne smiled warmly. "Yes. I'm Police Detective Anne Roget. How may I help you?"

"My computer isn't working."

"Oh. Did anything unusual happen just before your computer went out?"

Frank thought about the "eat me" message and decided not to mention it. "It worked when it was working, then it wasn't."

"What kind of work do you do, Dr. Harvey?" She obviously knew the answer as she called him doctor. She streamed down a list of icons looking for the object he needed.

"I was trying to buy some groceries."

Garland spoke quietly into Anne's shoulder. She gave him a bewildered look.

"Huh? This is interesting." She turned back to Frank. "I'll be in touch." Anne hung up.

Frank looked at Cy as Cy ate a piece of toast.

"Want some?" Cy asked. Cy held up a plate with another buttered slice on it.

Chapter 21

The police station where Network Services was housed, located in the old downtown library, was sixteen miles from the dome, however it was only an eight minute ride from the downtown train station to the dome's train station. Anne looked toward where she knew her six-story facility to be in the distance.

"Pierce called ahead," Anne said to Garland, emphasizing the personal nature of her relationship with Wagner. They were only allowed entry to the dome's gateway because of the unusualness of the situation. Still the guard was wary. He checked their police credentials and did a voice and heart scan.

When she called, Pierce had also given her a hard time. He didn't want to allow them inside. It took some work to convince him that this system failure was nothing ordinary. It was dangerous and unprecedented.

"The dome is smaller than I remember," Anne said, "more crowded."

"More boats than I thought," replied Garland. "Still I would do just about anything to live under the dome."

"You've never lived under the dome?" Anne thought she remembered seeing a young Garland when she was in basic training.

He had that sly look he sometimes got and he didn't answer her. His glance darted around like a child in Wonderland. Anne didn't ask him what had happened. She doubted that Garland would tell her the truth anyway.

Instead she said, "Some people don't have the right temperament to live confined in a bubble. I didn't."

They walked down the pier and knocked on Frank's houseboat door. When Frank opened it, Anne gave Frank a winning smile.

Frank seemed disconcerted, shocked. Something weird had just happened. "I can't remember the last time I met someone new," he said. He smiled broadly at her.

"Hello Dr. Harvey. I'm Police Detective Anne Roget." A phone image contained her badge. She held it out for his inspection. "This is Officer Zach Garland. He's going to take a look at your computer while we talk, if that's okay."

Frank nodded and stepped aside for them to enter.

Anne looked over her records annoyingly slowly. She looked up at him. "Franklin Roosevelt Harvey, Ph.D., Botanist," she said.

Frank nodded.

"Franklin Roosevelt?"

"As an infant, I was left in a hospital waiting room in Hyde Park, New York – the birthplace of Franklin Roosevelt."

"Ironic, huh, that you were named for a president famous for relief and recovery during a great depression. And Harvey? Where did that come from?"

"Name of the hospital patient who found me."

"And then what?"

"I was owned by the state for eighteen years. Two emergency shelters and two foster care placements."

"You know all this, so why are you asking?" Frank wanted to know.

Anne ignored his question. "What happened there?" Anne asked. "At the first foster care?"

"They didn't want to foster any longer. They gave me back."

Anne again looked at her records. "The Hogar family from age ten to sixteen."

"Even I will admit that I was acting out a bit."

"Then what?"

"I ran away, but got caught here in Austin. Emergency shelter until I aged out. After I was sprung, I attended college on a state scholarship."

"Scholarship that went all the way to a Ph.D.?"

"I worked hard," Frank said.

Anne's eyes traveled back to her notes "Wife," she said. "Etta Jane Harvey and son, Alexander Franklin Harvey. Huh."

"Yes," Frank said.

"So, what have you figured out so far?" Anne asked. She walked around Frank's living room and checked out his belongings.

"That's your job. I don't know."

"Hmm. You must have some thoughts."

"Network Services," Frank changed the topic avoiding her question. He looked piqued at her intrusion into his space. "That's crimes against machines," he said.

"It's never about the machines." Anne plopped on Frank's sofa. She picked up his sketchbook and flipped through it. "Nice," she said.

Frank took the drawing pad from her and put it in the top drawer of his desk. He sat in the desk chair.

"I don't have enemies," Frank said. "I live a quiet life."

"You grow and distribute food," she said. "Is that right?

"Yes."

Short answers, no information. There's a technique her training officer once taught her. If a man asked you if you have a blue shirt, you never said yes, I have a blue shirt and a red one and a purple one. You just said yes, I have a blue shirt. It seemed that Frank agreed with that school of thought.

"What kind of food?" she asked.

"All kinds: tomatoes just came in, and we have some nice catfish in a hatchery."

He glanced at her hands. She realized that she was twisting her wedding band on her left ring finger. She forced herself to stop.

"So, you sit at your computer and decide who gets to eat and who doesn't." She kept her voice quiet and pleasant, even when her sentiment was not.

"I don't make the decisions about where the food goes. The Wagner Company keeps tight control."

Garland put up a screen on Frank's wall.

"Oh," Anne said, "You're up and running again."

Garland moved to Anne's side and whispered into her left ear. "His accounts are zeroed out." It took a moment for the truth of what Garland was saying to sink in.

"But here's the thing, something odd." She turned back to Frank. "All your data is missing. Dr. Harvey, you're wiped."

"What? What's that mean?" Frank jumped up and flicked his Nomad. "Screen One. Show Bank Account." The screen came up for the bank, but he couldn't log in.

"It's as if you don't exist, as if you have never existed."

"But I'll get my money back, right? You can restore?"

"What money? I don't know what's true."

Frank looked stunned. It was time for her to hit hard. Anne leaned forward. "You're a very forward-thinking man, Dr. Harvey. Houseboat. Food commodities. Starvation is still the number one cause of death. People are afraid to be hungry again. They're afraid of a second famine."

Frank didn't respond.

"You have a wife…"

"Ex-wife."

"…and a son on the outside. What about them? How are they doing?"

"Same as everyone else."

Frank slumped back into his office chair. He had shut down.

"What's that mean? Same as everyone else."

He didn't respond. He sat in his desk chair fiddling with his useless Nomad, desperately trying to find his data. He was not going to answer any more questions.

Anne and Garland left. As they reached the gateway, Anne nodded to Garland. He took a position just outside the gate where he could watch Frank's houseboat.

Chapter 22

Anne removed the hood on her sunsuit and raised her hand to protect her eyes from the sun's burning rays. She noticed a path beaten into Etta and Alex Harvey's dusty front yard. Anne placed her feet, one after the other, on the trail until it abruptly ended at a split and fallen tree—half of which leaned on the house from the ground to the Harvey's roof. She pushed off the ground and shimmied up the tree, holding tight to the trunk.

She was breathing hard, sweating once she reached the roof. The tree had been moved a couple feet to one side and there was a door folded against the roof like a basement or root cellar door with a solid padlock sealing it. She knocked. No answer. She gave it a couple good tugs. When it didn't give, she worked her way back down the tree.

At the front door, she knocked again. No one was home. Anne knew Alex's mother was ill, so she didn't expect to find the house empty. Anne picked the old-fashioned tumbler lock and stepped inside.

Anne looked at the happy family picture over the entryway table. Etta was roundly pregnant. Anne thought this was probably the last time the family was healthy and whole.

Anne had become fascinated by Franklin Harvey and by extension his family. She had pulled together a file of interesting facts from Repository records. First, Anne recognized Etta as the doctor who tried to help her husband at the gate as he died. When she saw Alex's photo, she recognized him as the boy from the train station roof who did drawings of the dead. If the teen was Etta's son, then he was also the boy whose hand she held at the train station. Anne had a personal connection to all the members of the Harvey family.

One other thing she had pieced together, Etta had developed a serious kidney infection during the pregnancy pictured in the painting, resulting in a premature delivery and the death of her baby. Etta's doctor thought the kidney infection had been the result of sex with a person infected with gonorrhea. Anne could see how that situation could lead to all kinds of marital strife. It wasn't surprising they had divorced not long after that.

Anne stepped into the living room. Clearly, Etta and Alex had not done well during the Famine. This was surprising, since Alex's father was a Vice President at the Wagner group. There was a well-worn sofa, an old teak console table, simple in its lines, and a matched pair of lamps. That was pretty much all this room now contained. There was space for a dining table, chairs, even a buffet, but none existed. There was no grate in front of the old wood-burning fireplace, but plenty of evidence of fires. Anne placed the warrant to search the premises on the table.

An island separated the living room from the kitchen with its outdated, but functional appliances. She opened the refrigerator. Inside were a peach and a jar of tea. She sniffed it and smelled honey. Anne checked the cabinets. They were cluttered with little glass jars, smaller than baby food jars. Many were filled with dry leaves. But there was very little food: a box of crackers and three cans of soup. There were, however, plants in the kitchen window. Anne recognized some herbs like sage and basil. She sniffed one. Mint. Yum.

Anne glanced out the kitchen window onto a back deck. A pergola covered a ten-by-twenty-foot area. Its sides were made up of vertically ascending planters filled with herbs, some savory and some probably medicinal. She opened the door and the smell of the mint was intoxicating, and something else; anise, it smelled like anise. Did that even grow in this part of the world? She didn't know.

Anne stepped outside. The diffused light in the enclosed area made the porch a cool 99 degrees, according to a wall thermometer. Just beyond the porch, the sun was blaring. She saw the remains of a large garden, maybe something close to a quarter acre. Next to a wooden planting stand were two Adirondack chairs. Anne could picture Frank and Etta sitting in the chairs watching the plants grow in the several raised beds that now mostly contained piles of bleached dirt. At one end were a series of poles strung with rope mesh. Crawling on the mesh were the withered remnants of some kind of vine. Curled at the bottom of a twelve-foot water tower was a hose, brittle from lack of use.

She went back inside.

She moved down a dark hall toward the back of the house. The first bedroom had a hole from the fallen tree covered, she assumed, by the door on the roof. The craggy edge of the hole had been neatly repaired on the inside with planks of finished teak that matched the entryway table. Anne guessed that this was a piece of furniture, maybe the dining table, sacrificed for that purpose.

A mattress, box fan and four or five plastic bins were on the floor. One of the bins was open so Anne started her search with that one. Clothes, mostly dresses. In the third bin down, she found baby clothes, many with the price tag still on, a brand new stuffed monkey and a well-worn panda. There was a wedding photo of Frank and Etta and another of Frank, Etta and a third person riding bikes on a wooded trail. The extra man looked remarkably like a fit, young Charlie Broadnack. A small box contained a dozen pictures of a baby-faced Alex. There was also a photo of a woman posing next to a baby elephant. There were letters, three or four, from an address in the Sahara. Anne had her own box of Nathan's favorite things in her bedroom. Anne thought she would like Etta Harvey.

The remaining bins produced nothing of significance: towels and shoes and one bin of remarkably smelly sheets. There were a few more mementos, maybe from her parents or grandparents.

Next, Anne peeked into the bathroom. Not much there. She noticed a rich, floral scent and touched the shower curtain to ensure that someone had not just taken a shower. Dry. The scent didn't seem to fit either Etta or Alex. Maybe Alex had a girlfriend.

Yes, he did. A charcoal drawing of a pretty, young girl filled the space over Alex's bed. It was black and white, except for a flourish of yellow-red hair. A Bill of Rights, written in an old-fashioned calligraphy, lay on a table. Anne had heard of this new Bill of Rights, but she had never seen it. She read it carefully. Anne thought about what the Bill of Rights might mean to Alex – rights, fairness and justice.

The things in people's private spaces always told so much about what was important to them. She thought about her own apartment. One whole wall was a photo wallpaper of a North Carolina beach and on the wall opposite hung a dozen pictures of Nathan. No one ever saw that. Her office had one picture of

Nathan, but that was all. She guessed that said something too. She valued her privacy.

Alex's room had a bed, a desk and a dresser. The furniture thief was hesitant to hit this room. But, it was also bare. Anne looked in the closet. Off-season clothes. Two skateboards and a pogo stick littered the floor. It showed a physicality Alex shared with his father. Frank's house had been littered with hand weights, running shoes and stinky socks.

Only the disturbed dust told of a laptop computer that was no longer there. She fingered through the desk and found an odd assortment of drawings, notes and diagrams, a few of which she put into her bag. Anne crawled around on the floor, covering every inch with her hands. Her first find was an empty condom wrapper and then she was rewarded with a flash drive buried in a crack against the floorboard, almost under the desk.

"Huh," Anne said.

She opened her bag and pulled out her laptop. She plugged in the drive. A moment too late, it occurred to her that this might be a copy of the virus Alex had used to wipe his father's accounts, but it wasn't.

"How did you get this, smart boy?" Anne asked the air. She had clearly underestimated Alex's talents.

Chapter 23

Sheala O'Dell, Alex's high school teacher, ushered the last of her kids out the door. Anne showed her badge and Mrs. O'Dell stepped aside to allow Anne to enter her classroom.

Mrs. O'Dell displayed moving pictures on each of the four walls of the room. Anne examined them. The chronology seemed to begin with the election in the Year 2000. The teacher editorialized in a caption that implied if Al Gore had become president with his environmental agenda, things might have turned out differently, but Anne thought not.

On another wall, a video on continuous loop called "Early Warning Signs" showed images from hurricanes Katrina and Sandy, the heat waves in the southwest, the 2012 tornado outbreak and Northeast blizzard of 2013, extreme weather that went through the tsunami on the east coast in 2025. And so on.

On the flip side, people responded by recycling, buying hybrid cars and low-flow toilets, as if that would be enough to turn the tide of simultaneous disasters. It was way past too late.

And then the global economy collapsed. While a few individual intranets like theirs survived in isolated communities, the global Internet was shut down. Information was hoarded, not shared. Resources were hoarded, not shared.

Ultimately the second global pandemic starting in 2025, called J-flu, stopped travel altogether. Each community kept to its own, curbing the tide of migration and therefore the spread of disease.

When she was young, Anne's family had traveled from suburb to city, from east to west, all over the United States, looking for the best possible life. As isolation and illness grew, her family just happened to get stuck in Austin, Texas. Her dad had heard that the Wagner Company was hiring builders.

Anne looked at a poster on the teacher's door that the students had made: pictures and captions. Each student would see it every day.

Purposes of the Dome:

1. Collect, purify and cool water, with a picture of a big drop of cooling wet,

2. Protect crops from the sun, with an ear of corn growing in a field, and

3. Save the food chain, save fish in a flowing river.

The dome. The final step to total isolation, a tiny, blurry fishbowl.

"Mrs. O'Dell," Anne said.

"Call me Sheala."

Anne liked the respect that titles offered, especially with people older than herself, but she would do as asked.

"Sheala. You're teaching the Famine like it's history."

"For these kids, it is." Sheala sat in the teacher's chair behind her desk. She opened a ream of white paper and started writing out her next day's lesson.

"No," Anne said. "It's not."

"How can I help you today?" Sheala asked.

Anne pulled a student chair over to the teacher's desk.

"What can you tell me about Alex Harvey? He's your student, isn't he?"

"Sometimes."

"Meaning."

"Meaning when he shows up, which isn't often."

"He seems like a very bright boy," Anne said.

Sheala leaned in conspiratorially. "There's a lesson in the Repository about the building of the dome. As it nears completion, a shady, stealth figure sets an explosive that blows it up. Boom."

Anne smiled and quickly covered it up. "You think Alex did that?"

"It can't be done," Sheala said. "This history lesson, in fact all these teaching objects come straight out of the Repository. You would know better than I that you can't change an object in the Repository."

Shouldn't, not couldn't, Anne thought. "So what makes you think Alex's involved?"

"Alex's too smart for high school. I hear he spends his time with a professor at the university, some nutty old guy named Kolli Veddka."

"I've heard of him. Political. Radical."

"Yes. That's what he's teaching Alex," Sheala paused. "Alex's not a good influence on the other children. He riles them up, instigates them to do things they shouldn't do."

"Like what?"

Sheala pointed at the computer as if nothing more needed to be added. "He caused me no end of trouble."

"Can you say more?"

"Alex often didn't attend school and, when he was in class, he didn't take it very seriously."

"Can you tell me anything else useful?" When Sheala didn't answer, Anne nodded and moved toward the door.

"Alex." Sheala replied, "He's very angry."

Lost in thought, Anne exited the classroom and walked down the hallway. In her head, she reviewed her plan for investigation. Her Nomad signaled an alert, a message about something she was tracking. She pulled up the small screen. On her palm, she read.

Etta Jane Harvey, wife and mother of one son, died today of complications of kidney failure....

Anne sunk down the wall and propped herself against it. She couldn't move.

Chapter 24

It had only been a half-day since the police left, but Frank felt victimized, bedraggled and thinner already. He opened the door to his mini-refrigerator. Still, it held the Wasabi paste, a jar with a few olives and two slowly rotting limes.

In a cabinet, Frank slid aside the jar of Nutella and spied a half-full bottle of tequila at the back. He brushed away a coating of dust and mouse droppings, grabbed the bottle and headed out his front door.

In the waning light of evening, he walked past the last houseboat toward the end of the pier. In this last five-hundred square foot pod, two people sat in a flicker of blue light as if in a trance, numb, eyes forward. Frank sat down at the end of the pier with his feet hanging over the edge, upping the bottle again and again.

When the dome was secured, they had made one huge mistake. They weren't thinking about the hydroelectric workings of the turbine that controlled the release of overflow water from the reservoir to the river basin. These controls were in a secure building outside the dome on the other side of the dam. The powerhouse which housed the controls from which the turbines were operated was easy enough to access from the outside, but the dome was built to the edge of the dam, cutting off access from the inside. Frank and his crew routinely needed to reach the turbines for maintenance of underwater parts that didn't tend to have a long lifespan. He and his assistants cut a gate from the inside of the metal grate that filled a hollow space just above the edge of the dam to just below the edge of the dome. This allowed a man to walk across the top the dam and then take a ladder on the outside down a narrow service shaft to the door to the turbines in the Powerhouse.

Frank tossed the cap of the tequila bottle into the iron mesh gate and watched it dance on electricity before it fell to the water. They hadn't asked permission from Wagner when they put in this gate to the outside world. It wasn't meant to be a secret, just a practical way to get the job done, but Wagner electrified it along with the exterior of the dome, thereby making it useless.

The next morning, Frank woke on his sofa with a headache. The tequila, the limes and the olives were gone. He stared at the half-empty jar of Nutella.

Frank left his house and walked over to knock on Cy's door. Cy opened the little window in his door.

"I was wondering if I could take you up on that offer for a piece of toast," Frank asked.

"That toast is toast." Cy shut the little door.

Frank ambled slowly down the pier toward his hydroponics farm. He strolled up to the farmer who worked in the peach orchard. He could see a peach hanging large and plump on the limb of the tree. It was almost in reach.

"Hey. How you doing? Nice day out." Frank reached out his hand to shake with the farmer.

The farmer nodded. He indicated the dirt on his fingers.

"I'm Dr. Frank Harvey." Frank couldn't tell if the farmer recognized his name.

"I know that," he finally said.

"You're doing a great job here. Just great."

"Thanks."

"I'm head botanist here."

"I know," the farmer said. "We've met a bunch of times."

"I would like to sample one or two of those peaches. You know, like a quality check."

"Sure." The farmer wiped his hands on his pants and pulled out his Nomad. He waited. "You got one of those hand things?" he finally asked. He spread his fingers wide to show the fleshy part where Frank's chip would be.

Frank held out his hand. The farmer swiped it, but it did nothing. "I have a number. Twenty nine, seventy six."

The farmer plugged in the number then shook his head. "You know you have to have proper authorization."

"Here's the thing," Frank said. "Someone wiped my accounts."

"How could someone do that? It's not even possible. Just call Network Services and get them to restore."

Frank had no reasonable response for that.

The farmer shook his head again. "I tell you what. If you can say my name, I'll buy you this peach."

"John"

"No."

"James."

The farmer turned away. He was done.

Without thinking Frank made a lunge past the farmer for the peach. The farmer twisted out of the way, and Frank fell to the ground from a jolt.

"Have you lost it?" Alarm was clear in the farmer's voice. "There's a safety grid around the trees. You know that."

Frank hung his head and walked off. He held up his mobile device. "Check balance."

"Your account shows a balance of zero dollars," the computer answered in a friendly voice.

Frank walked the orchard path in circles with no particular destination. He was within arms-length of food that was just beyond his touch. He had to do something. He needed to take action. "Call Broadnack."

Charlie Broadnack, big man in his underwear, responded. Charlie had a 2D and a 3D screen up behind him. The weather was on the 2D screen. The radar showed nothing but the same field of pale green, except for a small sliver of yellow in the top right corner.

"Same as yesterday. Same as tomorrow," the forecaster predicted.

On the 3D screen, Charlie played video golf. He lined up a putt that he missed.

"Hello Charlie."

Charlie casually put on his shirt.

"I've got a bit of a problem. My account is zeroed out."

"Zero you say. How's that possible?"

"Police are working on it, but I need..."

"Police?" Charlie interrupted, alarm in his voice.

"I need food until this gets sorted out."

Charlie looked unnerved. "What do you expect me to do?"

Frank wanted to yell. "Use the FFEA account," Frank said.

"I've stuck my neck out for you. Done things for you that endangered my job, but no more. I'm done doing favors for you."

Charlie hung up before Frank could respond. Frank kicked out at nothing like a discordant kickboxer in a fight with himself.

He headed home.

Frank used his fingers to dig into the jar of Nutella then licked them. He wiped them on his pants when his Nomad signaled.

"Anything?" Frank asked, recognizing Detective Roget.

"Dr. Harvey," Anne said. "I wish to talk to you about something that's happened. It's very important. I'd like you to come to the downtown police station please. I've arranged for a pass?"

"Why? What happened?"

"I'll expect you in about an hour."

"No. Wait." But she had hung up.

Frank called Wagner's office. A blonde woman slithered into the back rooms and shut the bookcase as Wagner responded.

"We have an appointment?"

"No. It's just... I need..."

"Spit it out, man."

"The police have ordered me downtown. Can they do that?"

"No. I'll take care of it."

In a few minutes, Wagner called him back. He was a bit too red in the face.

"You better go," he said.

Frank stood under the protection of his covered front deck. He studied the row of houseboats tied to the long pier.

"Man up," he told himself.

He applied sunscreen to his face and put on a pair of dark sunglasses. He pulled a pair of metallic, protective pants to his waist and slipped on a metallic jacket. He pulled the hood over his head.

Cy came out onto his porch.

Frank stepped out from under his overhang. He looked up at the cloudless sky through the tinted dome. The sun was blurred.

Frank looked at Cy, but did not speak. He walked down the pier.

At the gateway, two biodome guards watched Frank as he approached. With trepidation, he finally reached the gate and they did a digital scan.

One guard checked his ID online. "Lift your hood," he said.

Frank revealed his face. He breathed out with relief that at least this part of his identity had been restored.

The guard looked skeptical even as the gate slid open. So did Frank. Outside he saw the covered light rail train station.

"How long since you've been out?"

Frank responded, "ten years."

The Number One train for downtown pulled into the station and Frank stepped on.

Chapter 25

Frank sat in a nearly vacant train car. Outside the window, he saw the power plant through the dome. The train followed the river until it changed direction. Suddenly, it was dry, barren and rocky. Where once trees lined the route, now one spindly juniper struggled to survive. A fire smoldered in the distance as cargo planes dropped retardant.

Frank sweltered in his sunsuit and pulled off his hood. Another rider took off his headgear as well. The rider had sores from skin cancer on his face and neck. His eyes were vacant, empty. Frank turned away.

When he left the downtown train station, Frank put on dark glasses. He raised his hood and walked down the street, sweating buckets in his metallic sunsuit.

Emaciated people lined up at the barred and metal door of a little grocery depot between an abandoned dry cleaner and a small pharmacy. The store's sign said "Wagner Company Store – Section 7." He recognized the number.

A fight broke out in line just as he opened the door. Warily, Frank inched by them and slipped inside.

Inside, the store was dark. The shelves had a few items in cans and sealed containers. Behind a counter was a refrigerated room. Sam, the middle-aged, burly grocer, exited the refrigerated room carrying a crate of peaches. Sam set them on the counter and began to hand them out. Frank noted the paltry amount, not nearly enough for the line outside. Not nearly as many as Frank had sent.

"One at a time mates. Queue up. Only one per customer. You know the rules."

Sam recorded a number into his Nomad, and then handed out a peach, over and over again. Frank waited for the peaches to be gone. It didn't take long, and then he stepped up to the counter.

Sam nodded.

"You know who I am?" Frank asked.

"Sorry."

"I sent you those peaches. I head food distribution for the Wagner Company."

Sam's expression turned sour. "And what will you be wanting now?"

"I set up an account called FFEA?"

"Excuse me?"

"I want you to give me some food from that account."

Sam disappeared back into the refrigerator. He came out with half a loaf of bread and a small hunk of ham. "You must be daft," Sam said as he sliced the ham.

"Check your records," Frank responded.

"I don't need to. I remember the account. FFEA. Food for Etta and Alex, that right?"

Frank nodded.

"I lost access to that account in the first few weeks. Far as I know, it doesn't exist anymore."

"What? That's impossible. I've been sending food to my family for ten years."

"Not to my store."

Sam loaded some ham between two slices of bread. "Sorry mate. Look around. Does it look like I'm running the Black Market?"

"What's that account have to do with the Black Market?"

Sam shrugged his shoulders. He took in Frank's hungry stare and held out the sandwich. "I'll take those fancy sun shades in exchange."

Frank handed over his sunglasses, took the sandwich and left the store. He walked through a park eating the sandwich. He watched a gardener pushing an old push mower across the dirt. The gardener wagged a pointed finger at him.

"You best be careful with that."

Frank heard the snarling before he saw them. Three relentless beasts, what used to be family dogs, were on him, yipping and stinking. One dog, his yellow canines dripping, ripped the hem of Frank's jacket. Frank kicked that bag of ribs half a block away.

He turned on the other two dogs, hands up like a monster and yowled in return. The dogs backed off for a few seconds, but then came again. It gave him the time to run. Had the dogs not been weak and he in shape they would have caught him before he got three blocks.

Frank tossed the sandwich behind him as he ran. It gave him another minute to dash down the street to the door of Charlie Broadnack's apartment tower. As he escaped inside, the dogs jumped on the glass door, teeth bared, slathering saliva.

Chapter 26

Inside. Safe. Frank had escaped the dogs. His heartbeat raced. He ran down a lushly carpeted hallway as if he were still being chased. He took the elevator to the fourteenth floor. He pushed a doorbell. It took a minute for Charlie Broadnack to answer.

"Harvey," he said. "You're out of your bubble. I didn't think you had it in you." He stumbled to one side to allow Frank to enter.

Charlie was disheveled despite his attempt to look grand in a silk, paisley bathrobe worn hanging open over sweat pant bottoms with holes in the knees.

Frank pulled off his sunsuit jacket. He walked directly to the kitchen sink and turned on the water. Frank splashed his face with it and cupped his hands for a drink.

Charlie took a swig from a nearly empty bottle in his hand. He had been blowing up balloons. He laid a red balloon on a heavy oak table. The balloon was dangerously close to a humidor and an ashtray with a lit, half-smoked cigar. The patio door was open and a stale, hot wind pushed the red balloon closer to the ashtray. Frank shut the door.

The scene felt odd: balloons, cake, cigar and whiskey. These were all things not available. Not available to him, he amended. Frank surveyed the room as he collapsed into a comfy overstuffed chair.

Charlie picked up his cigar, waved it around and then put it back in the ashtray.

Frank ran his finger through the icing on the cake and licked it off. He got up and cut himself a slice.

"Remember Etta back when we first met? She had the prettiest eyes," Charlie said. This seemed to be a continuation of a conversation Charlie had been having with himself, a conversation that Frank didn't want to have with Charlie.

"I don't know what I would have done if you hadn't helped Etta and Alex."

Charlie stared at Frank. A complex series of emotions crossed his unguarded expression.

The balloon on the desk popped and both men masked their startled jump. He had been expecting it, but was still surprised when the pop actually came.

"Today's my birthday," Charlie said. Did you know that?" Charlie took another swallow from his bottle, gulping it down. "I have plans, very permanent plans." He struggled to get up when there was a knock at the door. Frank stood as well.

"I'll get it," Frank said. He opened the door to Anne. She walked past him. "What are you doing here?" he asked. It dawned on him that she must have had surveillance on him to get here so quickly. Him or maybe Charlie.

Anne looked around the room at Charlie, the balloons and the cake.

"You stood me up, Dr. Harvey," she said. "Must be for something very important." She looked at Charlie and flipped out her badge. "Police Detective Anne Roget. Happy birthday, Mr. Broadnack."

Charlie lumbered to his feet. "You have nice eyes, Anne. Very pretty."

"Thank you Mr. Broadnack."

"Charlie. Call me Charlie. Frank gets all the girls with pretty eyes."

"I would love it if you gentlemen would come downtown with me so we can chat."

"Both of us?" Charlie asked.

As they entered the police station, Charlie Broadnack leaned on both Anne and Frank. Anne dropped the unsteady man into a chair in an interview room.

She could see Garland in a room filled with older computer equipment. Through a window, Anne watched him curiously as he tapped on the keys. He hit the send button. Garland was up to no good. She knew it. She took a few steps back before she called out.

"Officer Garland."

Garland's head shot up as he exited his work.

"Show Dr. Harvey some pictures."

After Garland exited, Anne went to Garland's computer and ran a couple searches. She copied a few locked files to a jump drive to break open later.

Anne watched Garland in interview through the one-way mirror. Garland called up a series of mug shots. "These are known dissidents with high-tech know-how. Mostly, they're known for protests outside of the gate and small demonstrations of unruliness. I guess you wouldn't know about dissidents," Garland said.

"What do you mean?" Frank asked.

"What with living on the inside..."

Broadnack roused a bit. "Hey," he said. "Hey. Hey." He limply waved a finger in the air.

Garland ignored Broadnack and looked at a felon who was mugging it for the camera.

"I love this guy," Garland said. "You recognize him? I'd get a kick out of picking him up."

"You're not taking this very seriously."

Garland and Frank did a macho face-off, staring eye to eye. The screen changed without either of them paying attention. The next picture was a photo of a man in his thirties, young, healthy. The photo was labeled "Kolli Veddka."

"Hey," Broadnack said. "I know you."

Anne laughed at the interview from her position in the observation room. Garland seemed to feel her gaze on the back of his neck and directed his comment to the mirror.

"No, you don't."

Anne had been investigating the black market for months. Struggling with where to start, she had begun with people who had too much – too much power, too much food, too much fat on their bones. All roads led one place – to Pierce Wagner and his cronies. So what was the connection to an opportunistic young police officer?

Anne eased too fat, too rich Charlie Broadnack out the door of the interview room, leaving the door ajar. She directed him toward a folding chair. She gave him a glass of water and told him to stay. Charlie slumped a bit. Anne went back into interview.

"Dr. Harvey. Why was it more important to go see Mr. Broadnack than to keep your appointment with me?

"It was his birthday."

"Don't get snide with me."

"I was hungry. I thought Charlie might give me some food."

"I'm curious," Anne said. "Why didn't you go to your wife?"

"Ex-wife. She's mad at me"

Outside Interview, Charlie stirred in his hard chair when his mobile device rang. Charlie flicked a screen and Alex came on. "Hello," he said.

Alex was at the mortuary sitting opposite the funeral director. Rows of shelves filled with cheap cardboard boxes, like cake boxes waiting for their treats, lined the walls behind the director. "Charlie." Alex choked out the word.

"What's wrong? What happened?" Charlie was instantly alert and focused. It was as if any drink he'd had left his system disappeared.

"Mom," Alex fought with the word.

"What?" Charlie asked afraid of the answer. "Where are you?"

"I'm at the mortuary. I've made arrangements, but I need an adult to sign."

"I'll be right there."

Charlie caught the conversation in the interview room as he scrambled to his feet.

Anne spoke. "You talked to your wife this morning..."

"Etta asked me to help with..."

She interrupted. "And did you help her?"

"I couldn't."

Charlie reached the open door of the interview room.

"She wanted..." Frank started.

Charlie dragged Frank to his feet. "I don't care what she wanted," Charlie yelled. "Etta asked for help and you didn't help her." Charlie swung and Frank went down and out.

Charlie sunk to the floor. Anne found a handkerchief so Charlie could blow his nose. "I called dibs," Charlie said.

Chapter 27

Frank was sprawled, passed out on a cot in a small jail cell. Anne sat beside him on a stool. She leaned over. Her fingers lightly brushed a stray lock of Frank's hair from his forehead. He had a nice face. She liked his eyes too. His intelligence shined from behind them. She'd never met him when she lived under the dome, but she'd admired him from the security monitors. She especially loved watching him at work with his plants in the hydroponics farm or orchard.

"Etta?" Frank asked confused, not quite conscious. He opened his eyes, sat up too fast and rolled his aching head down into his hands.

"Dr. Harvey," Anne said.

"Is it blue?" Frank rubbed his stiff jaw. "I've never been in a fight before. Do I have something to show for it?"

Anne smiled. "You haven't been in a fight yet and, yes, it's a lovely shade of violet."

"How long was I out?"

"Fifty minutes."

"Is Charlie still here?"

"No, but he'll be back." Anne waited until Frank's eyes cleared. "Tell me about FFEA," she said.

Frank hesitated for a minute, and then resigned with a sigh. "Food for Etta and Alex. When the gate was locked and I was inside and they were outside, I set up a special account to make sure that Etta and Alex had the things they needed."

"And what happened to it?"

"I don't know. I just found out today that it was shut down. Been closed for a decade."

"You had to have help on the outside," Anne queried.

"I can't tell you that," Frank said.

"It was Charlie," Anne said.

Frank didn't respond.

"I've been reviewing some interesting files. I can prove Charlie sold your FFEA account to the Black Market, but I don't know who he sold to."

"But why?"

"It was an easy-to-access, illegal method for distribution that was already established and the one person likely to catch the fraud would probably look the other way. "

Frank rubbed his temple. "Charlie has his flaws, but I never thought he would steal from Etta or Alex."

"You haven't talked much to your friend lately, have you?" Anne asked. She watched as Frank stood and paced the cell. "Despite everything, Charlie took care of your family. He brought them food, helped with their basic needs."

Frank's face looked stunned. "Charlie sold the account I set up to provide Etta and Alex with food? I know Charlie provided them with scraps, but I always thought this was additional to what I provided. Charlie took credit for taking care of them?" he repeated.

"He's been unhappy since the breakup with Etta." Anne twisted her wedding ring. "

"Why?"

"Tell me about Etta." He hesitated. "Please, Dr. Harvey. I'd love to know more about your family."

"I'd rather you tell me about your family."

"My husband is dead." Anne said it flatly with a touch of angst.

"I'm sorry," Frank's voice went soft. He moved closer to Anne, lowered his voice making it more intimate. "Etta has a sister who was unable to travel during the pandemic. She was stuck in North Africa."

"So when the gate was electrified, you had no other family and she did."

"Yes."

"So she stayed out and you went in."

"Something like that. It wasn't that simple. It all happened so fast."

"And then Etta got ill and Alex was stealing so the two of them might survive."

"Wait. What? Alex was stealing?" Frank said. "When our relationship could still be repaired, he begged me to come home, but by then...."

"What happened?"

Frank clammed up while Anne patiently waited. Frank changed the subject.

"I don't understand why Charlie would be so upset about my breakup with Etta. Why would he care?"

"I wasn't talking about your divorce," Anne said. "I was talking about Charlie and Etta's recent split."

Frank was surprised. "So he finally won. It's what he always wanted."

"Dr. Harvey," she said. "I'm very sorry to have to tell you that your ex-wife succumbed to starvation this morning. She's dead."

Frank started to shake. "No. That can't be. I talked to her today. She seemed fine." He gasped in dry heaves. "A little under the weather, she said."

Anne waited for him to catch his breath. "She suffered kidney failure brought on by long-term anemia."

"She would have told me if she needed help."

"Didn't she?"

Frank didn't respond.

"I'm releasing you. Go take care of your son."

Chapter 28

Outside his house, Frank looked at the wreck of a car, the sinkhole in the street and the split, fallen tree. As he neared the entry, he saw the red door and a panel of prickly pear cactus in a rusted tin can, wild with bloom. Tears rushed his eyes.

It was gloomy and hot as he entered the house. Frank flipped on a light in the living room. He checked the air conditioner. It didn't work. He looked around at Etta and Alex's meager belongings. All gone, except the sofa, now tatty, and the family picture in the hallway. The entry table had been moved to behind the sofa and the two table lamps sat on it, but none of the kitsch that had made this house their home was there.

Frank heard the slide, and then a slam and a crash. He rushed to the window in Alex's room in time to see Alex jump onto and then tightrope walk down the thin edge of the fence. Alex flipped and ran down the street away from the house. He ran two blocks in the blink of an eye.

Frank rushed out the front door to follow Alex, but Alex was a ghost.

"Alex," he yelled into the air. "Let me help." No response.

Frank went back into the house to Alex's room. He saw books, lots of books, music. A superman action figure lay on the floor. Frank stared at a drawing of a red-haired girl on the wall. Pretty, but she made Frank sad for all the things he missed.

He looked out the door, across the hall. He went and stood by the door to Etta's bedroom. He held his breath. His hands shook.

Inside, he saw her mattress on the floor, but Etta was not there. He saw the boards nailed to the ceiling to cover a rough hole and the box fan near the window.

There was a storage box that contained some of Etta's belongings standing open by the bed. Frank sat on the floor by the box and looked through the items. He found a current picture of Alex. He discarded the frame and pocketed the photo.

He was about to stand when he noticed the red dress in the box that Etta had worn as he tried to drag her through the train station to the gateway of the dome – and failed. He bowed his head and sobbed.

After the sun fully set, Frank walked aimlessly.

The outside world was different at night. He saw a man working in the dim light of his little greenhouse. The man nurtured his growing plants with care just like Frank would have done. He caught Frank's stare and lowered his eyes not wanting to appear threatening.

Instead of being angry, the man said, "Plants. Aren't they beautiful? How they grow and adapt and change."

"I've always thought so," Frank responded. "How do you have enough water? I know your allocation won't do it. That's barely enough to take a shower once a week and have a drink every day."

"We don't shower. We take baths."

"We?"

The gardener spread his arms to indicate everybody. "We take baths, then when we're done, the neighbors put their bath water in the rain barrel and I use it to water the plants."

"Smart. Inventive," Frank said. "I did something like that at my house..." Suddenly he wasn't sure how to finish. He just said, "once."

A couple, dressed for a party, exited their front door. The woman wore a red blouse with a scarf on her shoulders that glittered. She carried an oversized brocade fabric bag that reminded him of Etta's. The man had a guitar slung across his back. He took the bag from her and shouldered it. They smiled and waved to Frank. Frank followed them down the street.

"Going to the Park?"

Frank nodded although he had no idea what that meant.

The man stuck out his hand to shake. "Kai and Greta Van de Vliert," he said.

"Frank Harvey," he responded.

The three of them cut through a fence around a yard. Two men patted his chest and pockets as he entered what looked like a farmer's market on the lawn of a Victorian house. The market was quite invisible from the street. One of the guards looked up at a third man in a crow's nest on top of a pole. The third man gave a nod and he was allowed entry.

Makeshift booths made of folding tables or crates with vendors who operated them were set up on either side of a path. There was a crowd of people who strolled from booth to booth buying, trading and sharing their wares.

Frank saw Greta pull something out of her bag. It was wrapped in cloth. She handed it to a vendor. The vendor uncovered a fresh loaf of bread and Greta gave it a satisfied sniff. In return, he handed her two huge bags of spinach. Greta stuffed the spinach into her brocade bag and moved on to the next vendor.

Frank walked from booth to booth. There were fruits, vegetables, jams, breads and eggs as well as candles, soaps and quilts—anything that people could grow or make.

There were family units in the park: mother, father and children. Frank sat at a bench and watched a father and son. The son wrapped his arms around his father's legs.

Frank wondered what he wanted from his own son, what would be the best outcome of a reconciliation. He remembered a day when he had taken Alex and his friend to the park and they played on the monkey bars. He remembered the way Alex laughed. He thought what he wanted from Alex might look like that.

Frank walked up to the man from the couple. "If you were a sixteen-year-old boy, where would you be tonight?"

Kai pointed. Under the lights in the trees, people were gathering with instruments. They tuned up guitars and violins. Five women sang a few lines without accompaniment, their voices intricately blended, then the drums came in, a dozen of them – driving a beat. Frank hadn't heard live music in years. He sat on the bench and listened, his eyes glassy.

Frank watched the people. He could see the physical and psychological wounds on their faces. But they ran to each other, hugged and touched. They danced, swayed to the music holding each other at the waist. There was something whole. He couldn't quite put his finger on it at first, but then it came to him. It was joy.

Ultimately, he got up and started walking around showing Alex's photo at random.

"Have you seen this boy? He has shaved his hair off now."

Person after person shook his or her head no.

"He has the most spectacular green eyes," Frank noted.

They patted his arm knowing the sadness behind such a question. Frank felt overwhelmed. He'd almost given up.

A woman lifted the photo from his hand and stared at it. "Yeah," she said. I've seen him hanging out down by the train station near the entrance to the dome."

He waved to the young couple as he took off down the street.

He hadn't been walking for five minutes when, starting with the gate, the lights went out on the power grid, section by section, until the dome went black. The lights of the city also flickered, dimmed and died. Everything was eerily dark. Black.

Chapter 29

Anne wanted to scream. She was more affected by Etta Harvey's death than any since her husband. Etta was the beautiful doctor who had fallen to her hands and knees and tried to save Nathan. Anne wanted to breathe life back into Etta, as Etta had tried to breathe life back into Nathan when the dome's electricity stopped his heart.

Anne stood in front of a virtual white board. The box at the top for the perpetrator of the black market waited to be filled. This person killed Etta the same as if he'd strangled her. And she wasn't the only one. He denied food to the people who desperately needed it while giving it to people who could pay. Anne made a Victim box and put Etta's morgue picture in it. Etta was laid clean and calm on a cold metal table, ready for transport to the pyre. The Perp box was blank, but in her mind, she saw Wagner's picture there—self-absorbed, selfish and slightly sodden with single-malt whiskey.

She glared at Garland. Wishing she could take action, but she didn't have enough proof of wrongdoing yet. Garland was back at his desk furiously keying into his computer. He had this self-satisfied look on his face. He'd done it, whatever it was.

A network alarm sounded, shrill in the silence of the room.

"Could somebody get that?" She looked around the room, but, apart from Garland and her, nobody else was there. Just the same, the alarm stopped. Pulling objects from the Repository to replace corrupted ones was an easy job that could be done at home, so that's where most people worked.

Another alarm sounded. Then a third. Anne picked up the next call. She wanted to know what was going on.

She looked toward Garland with a suspicious, horrified and angry scowl, but he was gone. He had slipped out the door.

In a few minutes, it was evident things were going terribly wrong at Network Services. Five uniformed police officers rushed in from who knows where to respond to the incessant calls. Anne watched *their* look of confidence shrivel away as answers could not be found. Behind the clamor, a loud alarm rang. The noise was daunting.

"Disconnect that alarm. I can't think," she shouted. This time, someone responded.

A screen was up with the news. After the alarm was cut, the report could be heard.

"...failures of unprecedented scope," the newscaster said.

A fatal error message popped up on Anne's screen. She glanced at the other screens in the room. The same fatal error appeared on all of them.

"What is that thing?" June was a young policewoman who came in to assist with the overflow. June had a cautious, vulnerable temperament that made Anne feel protective of her. Maybe it was from being saddled by her parents with that moniker. Anne knew her first name was April. June's peers just called her Spring.

June wore tiny glass earrings, although jewelry was frowned upon, and a little pop of color on the tank top under her uniform. She had painted half of her short fingernails a bright red, obviously interrupted in the process.

"It's a warning," Anne replied. Anne touched June's arm to reassure her.

"We've got to get around it so we can get to the Repository," June said. The panic was just below her skin's surface.

"No. This message tells us something that we can't ignore."

"But objects are being damaged. We have to get new ones. If this goes on, we'll have nothing." Near hysteria was setting in. Anne took a minute to put her arm around June to comfort her. June quickly got hold of herself and pulled away. She stood tall with chin up. Anne was her superior and this wasn't cop behavior.

Over a couple of minutes, the activity in the room came to a standstill. No one got past the fatal error. It grew eerily quiet. Then the lights went out. Like the others, Anne rushed to the window and watched as the rest of the city flickered and died. Anne turned on a flashlight and looked from face to face. The half-dozen people in the near dark room stood and stared at each her.

"I guess we're done here. You should go home. Yeah," Anne addressed the larger room. "Go home to your families. Good night," she said.

June gave her a bewildered look, but walked out the door.

When it was quiet, Anne installed a battery in an old HP laptop computer and hooked up a flash drive. She bent over the keyboard as she started working again in the dark stillness. She scanned through the camera footage of the last few hours before the power went out. She activated a face recognition program.

"Find Alex Harvey – 2300 today."

The laptop scanned through the video data files on the backup hard drive and came back with a "Not Found" message. He must have had his Nomad dismantled when she'd copied the files to the drive.

"Find Frank Harvey," She looked at her watch, "thirty minutes either side of the same time."

The computer started with a wide view that narrowed as it chugged into focus on her screen. Frank was caught on camera at the gateway to the dome. Security had been amped up giving Anne an unsettled feeling of déjà vu. The guard station was bright, but as you moved away from the entrance, the space became more shadowed.

Frank waved a picture at the guards. "Did he go inside?" Frank asked. "Is he looking for me? He was seen around here." Frank struggled with the guards at the gate, attempting to force himself inside, but they pushed back. Frank was insistent and the guards were losing their patience.

"I just want to run in and check my houseboat for him. I don't have to stay. You can come with me. No problem."

"We're a bit busy here, moron." The guard said as he pushed Frank.

"But I live inside. There," Frank pointed. "He knows me. That's my neighbor, Cy."

Cy had a wheelbarrow from the hydroponics farm. How'd he get that? Anne wondered. The farm was protected.

"We're barricading the entrance," Cy said.

Anne noticed the crude wall of brick and mortar. The guard allowed Frank to take a few steps toward it. Frank was in, but he looked unsure.

The footage Anne was viewing no longer had a good view of Frank. She opened a second laptop. She only had a few minutes of battery life remaining. She needed to hurry. She searched through another set of files until she found some footage with a better view. From her new angle, Anne could see hordes gathering under the awning of the train station. The blurred walls of the dome allowed imaginations to go wild. More people drew together as she watched.

"They can't get in," Cy said emphatically.

The crowd began to chant, but the words were not clear. Anne could make out some words like "locked gate, sealed fate."

An elderly man with a walker came out of his houseboat. He stood at the door and yelled to the exterior crowd. "Go away. You're scaring my wife."

Cy and the others hauled odd bits of lumber and rock toward the entrance. "Give a hand, Harvey." The wall was already about waist high. Frank took one step inside.

But then Frank saw Alex just outside the dome wall. Hands only, Alex shimmied down a pole that ran along the side of the train station. He squared off to Frank, hands on his hips, on opposite sides of the dome. When it was clear that Frank had seen him, Alex turned his back on Frank and walked away.

"Alex. Wait. I'm coming," Frank called.

Alex disappeared into the crowd.

Frank ran to the gate and yelled to the guard. "That's my son," but it was a different security guard and this one pushed him back. "He's disappearing," Frank yelled, but no one seemed to care.

The improvised wall was growing. Frank pulled down wet bricks and debris. Cy went wild and lunged at Frank. Others joined in.

Anne switched back to the computer with the exterior footage and released it from pause. She saw Alex in the background. Alex watched as his father was tossed around like a rag doll by the dome guards. Anne was interested in whether Alex would intervene, come to his father's aid, but he did not.

As the city lights flickered and died, Alex disappeared into the dark night.

Realizing the power was off, Frank rushed the gate, but it was still locked with heavy iron bolts. He was sealed once again inside the dome.

Anne sat in the quiet and dark. This recording seemed to indicate that Alex was in the clear for this latest system failure.

Anne twisted her wedding ring on her finger and thought of Nathan.

Chapter 30

"How about North Carolina?" Nathan had asked one day shortly after they married. Nathan wanted to move. He thought the coast might be just the place to entice her. Anne had shared her memories of the beach with him. In hindsight, Anne could see he wanted to move anywhere not ruled by the Wagner Group. And that was way before the gate was locked.

Anne had a video of her family on vacation on the Crystal Coast of North Carolina, a chain of undeveloped barrier islands along the Atlantic shore. The toddler in the video played in the surf, riding the waves to shore again and again. She picked up shells on the beach while walking with her mother at sunrise.

Her family had rented kayaks and paddled over to Carrot Island. Anne rode tandem with her father in the little boat as it skimmed across the quiet surface of the sound. Passing sailboats gently rocked them in their wake.

On the far side of the island, they had passed near Sand Dollar Island where they saw the wild horses. First one, then three. Soon there were twenty or so. The chestnut horses stood in a shallow, swampy marsh surrounded by long-legged, white birds, some kind of heron maybe.

"It's in the wet," she had said. "It rains all the time there now." Anne looked it up online. The island had grown smaller. The water had risen by several feet from the constant rain. The rain washed out and covered up the grasses the horses had used as feed. The horses that had not drowned had to be removed to a safer, drier location. There were no horses on Carrot Island anymore.

Nathan didn't trust Pierce Wagner, but, at the time, Anne had closed her eyes to that. She idolized Pierce. To her, Pierce was a god who was building a solution when almost everyone else did little more than struggle to survive. And, she had been promoted twice. In essence, she'd become Nathan's commanding officer.

"It's just sour grapes," she had told Nathan. "That's why you dislike Pierce so much."

117

"Anne," he'd say. One of Nathan's famous one word answers, as if she should know what he thought. Now, more than once, she wished she had known what he was thinking. What had Nathan known that she did not? What had he believed?

After Nathan died, Anne had languished in her tiny, vacant apartment. She stared at the photo wall of Carrot Island as it had been when she was a child. Nathan had surprised her with it on their first wedding anniversary. She wished she'd gone with him to live at the beach. She'd sat on her deck all night, feeling fuzzy, groggy. She couldn't sleep and then didn't have the energy to stand up and go to work in the morning.

She had watched as goods were loaded onto the midnight train and sent to the kiosks to feed the town. In her head, she counted boxes. She watched as the train traveled the track to where it forked, sometimes going right, but often going left.

Eventually she had gotten up, she had gone back to work for Wagner Security and that's when she had wondered – "What's left?" Right was the town, the river where all people clung to life. Left was desert sand, too dry even for fire any more. Left was death.

Still in thrall with Pierce, she had stopped by his office and asked him, "What's to the left?"

Pierce had turned his wheels. She could see him attempting to formulate an answer. She'd thought it would be a simple question with a simple answer. She would ask where the rail ended and he would have a logical response, but she had known from his expression that anything that came out of his mouth would be a lie.

"We send a few things to the other end of the pipeline. They send back other things we need."

"You use our food to pay for what?" she had asked.

"Mostly other supplies."

"Supplies from Shreveport. Shreveport doesn't have anything to spare. They're more crowded than we are. How does this stuff get here? The tracks have been out for years."

"You wouldn't believe me if I told you."

"Try me." Anne had felt like she was enduring another death. She had tried to keep her face neutral and her voice even. "What do we get from them?"

"Don't you trust me?"

She didn't say what she was thinking. *Not at the moment.*

"Medicine," he had grasped for something she'd believe, something she'd care about, but Anne knew that there was no medicine. Not for her. Not for the insiders. And especially not for the outsiders.

"That's important," she said.

"Retardant," he had flowed with his story. "You wouldn't believe how much we spend on that red stuff to keep the fires at bay."

That's better, she thought. A better lie. Harder for her to track and disprove. "It must be doing a good job," she said. "The news reports that the fires have mostly burned themselves out. No fodder for the flames anymore."

Anne had looked around Pierce's office. She'd seen burned out cigars in his ashtray, a cabinet full of quality bourbon and fine wine. There was a bit of a chocolate wrapper in his trash, sloppily stashed under a wad of paper. These were the things that Pierce would take food out of starving people's mouth's to buy. There was no telling what Shreveport could acquire that Austin could not. Anne had decided to start a full-scale investigation.

Pierce could read faces too. Hers must not have been as neutral as she had hoped. Pierce had the look of ghosts in his eyes, a look that hid dark secrets.

"I've been thinking about something for a while now. I want you to move the police force outside the dome. It'll be easier to monitor the outsiders. I'll retain a small security force inside. Just a few guards. That's all we need. The crime isn't on the inside."

"Why?" Anne had asked in shock, but he didn't answer. "Fine," she said. That had been the day that Pierce lost his appeal. A day later Anne had been kicked out of the dome. The first thing she'd done was fill a backpack and take a walk along the train tracks out into the desert.

She had gone left.

Chapter 31

Next day, Anne went to the college. There was a wooden sawhorse standing as a barrier to the entrance. It had a sign that read "No Class Today." Anne climbed the stairs, moved the sawhorse and slipped through the ornate carved door.

The halls of the building were semi-dark and empty of people. Natural sunlight poured into the dim space from the one door left open. Anne stood at the door and watched an old professor, interrupting his thoughts as he stared out the window.

Anne gave him a double hard stare. The only picture she had seen of Kolli Veddka had been taken at least forty years before. This man had a button nose, doe eyes and long, scraggly, salt and pepper eyebrows. She thought that he could have had plastic surgery on the nose, worn brown contacts to hide his blue eyes, but it was unlikely that he would have added that ugly unibrow. She didn't think the professor was the guy they called Old Ved.

"Excuse me, Professor," Anne said.

He became only a silhouette as he turned to her with the light at his back.

"I'm looking for Ved." Anne showed him her badge and he examined it closely. She couldn't bring herself to call him "Old Ved" as many of her co-workers did.

"Professor Poutin."

"Professor Poutin?" Anne would have to look up that name.

"Yes, Professor Ved Poutin. Is that who you want? I'm sorry. I haven't seen him in the last few days. He's a very old man, dependent on a respirator." The professor shrugged to indicate that anything could have happened. "Did you try the hospital?"

"Actually, I'm looking for someone I think he knows. Alex Harvey."

"Ah. Alex, the prodigy."

"Shall we check his office?" Anne suggested.

"No security. I doubt I could stop you if I wished it." He escorted Anne to the door of Ved's office. Their footsteps echoed in the empty hallway. He unlocked the door.

Anne opened the door and let out a gasp. Books. Books everywhere. All over the desk, the floor and the table. Anne picked up one of the many books and began to read. She could tell how fragile and brittle these pages had become over a long period of time. She lay the book down gently, reverently.

"Why do you look for Alex Harvey?" the professor asked.

"I think he can help me."

"Not to arrest him?"

There was another table that held several different models of computers from all different stages of technology development. Anne saw a battery pack and picked it up. With the power out, she wanted to take it, but didn't.

"May I stay for a while?" She planned to wait for Alex no matter what this man said, but the old professor nodded and stepped back.

She searched through the books on the desk and selected two of interest. She set them on her lap and glided an office chair toward the window light.

When Alex entered Ved's office, Anne tensed and tried to appear normal. She didn't turn to notice him and he said nothing to her.

She had spread out over the desk going back and forth between several books and her notes. She'd pulled out her laptop and set it up, but had not turned it on to save the battery.

Alex cleared a space on a bookshelf, wiping it clean with his sleeve. From his canvas bag, he took out a cardboard box and gently set it on the shelf.

Anne said nothing about this, giving Alex space for his grief.

Alex walked to a long table and pulled a diagram from a hidden drawer that Anne had overlooked.

"Ved says that all the answers are on these bookshelves."

Anne turned to him. "I'm sorry about your mother. You must feel suddenly quite alone."

Alex walked to the window, his face lit by the sunshine through the glass.

"People can't make eye contact," Alex said. "No one talks about the famine. It's touched everyone's lives, but it's almost never addressed openly." Alex sat down opposite Anne and looked into her eyes.

"What would you say?" Anne asked.

"Recovery doesn't start until we quit ignoring each other's pain."

Anne appraised him. "That's quite a thing for a sixteen year old to say."

"I was taught well..." Alex picked up Anne's satchel and searched through it. "...by my mother." It contained mostly files and disks. Alex opened the paper file labeled with his name and skimmed it.

"Your teacher says that we are already in recovery," Anne said.

He pulled a peach from his messenger bag, twisted it and handed half to Anne. "You're investigating me. Why?"

"How long have you known Kolli Veddka?"

"Did my father sign a complaint against me?"

"Did you know Ved is considered a threat by the state?

"What did my father say?"

"Do you ever answer a question with an answer?"

"Do you?"

Anne sucked in a breath. "Someone," Anne paused for effect. "Someone has been tampering in the Repository. Someone has changed the data..." she waited for a reaction, "...and the code."

Alex looked down. "That's not possible. Just ask my teacher."

Anne nodded. "I've been trying to teach myself this language for about a year and a half. I," she emphasized the word, "I wasn't willing to take the risk of changing even one little thing. The code is riddled with bugs and traps. Something could happen by mistake," she paused. "Like a city-wide blackout."

"I didn't do it."

"A couple of things were really tripping me up," Anne said. "I thought all the files would be in one language, but they're not. The designers used lots of different databases and applications."

Alex tossed the peach pit and went to work at his computer. Anne looked over his shoulder to see.

"The other thing I thought is that when you went to get a replacement object in the library for say electricity that it actually turned on the lights. It doesn't. There is a separate program to do that. So nothing is actually wrong with the power, just the method by which the computer tells it how to operate."

Alex halted his rapid pace keying, the fastest Anne had ever seen. "Does that mean that the money is still in my father's account?"

"It's not so true of virtual things. You erased the data, not the program."

Alex nodded his understanding. All his father's money had ever been was the idea of a number in an account.

"I always thought of the Network as this miraculous thing, but it really doesn't work at all. It fails and then we recover. Over and over. We've forgotten how to really fix it."

Alex pulled a book from his canvas bag. "This one is very good reading," he said. "I found it particularly enlightening."

"Okay." Anne took the book into her hands. One of the pages was bookmarked. She opened to that page. "Ah," she said. "I could show you something." She glanced at the laptop battery sitting on the desk. "But I haven't the battery power."

"Unregistered standalone equipment is illegal."

"I've heard that. Surely some purposes are more important than a misdemeanor like that."

Alex flipped the top on a bin stowed under a table sitting in the corner of the floor. Inside, it was full of laptop batteries.

"Charged?" Anne asked.

Alex nodded.

"Did you know that the gate was never intended to be sealed?" Anne asked. "The dome was just a way to protect the food chain. It wasn't meant to separate the haves from the have-nots. There were horrible riots at the gate when security was first installed. Many people lost their lives for no good reason at all." Anne furiously twisted her wedding band.

"What was his name?" Alex asked.

"Nathan. His name was Nathan." She turned away from Alex as the tears welled up in her eyes. When she was in control, she turned back.

Alex appeared absorbed in reading a text, but she suspected he was giving her a moment.

"Before the gate was sealed, people died," she said, "but it wasn't murder."

"Murder?"

"We could have all lived with less, but when they sealed the gate, excluding the many so a few could live well..." she didn't finish her sentence.

"Are you thinking of helping me?" Alex asked.

"I'm thinking of helping everyone else. You're just a tool I'm thinking of using."

Alex lifted his eyes to her. He nodded.

From her pocket, Anne pulled out his flash drive. She handed it to him. "Something you've been working on?" she asked.

Chapter 32

Alex held his Nomad in the palm of his left hand. He stared at Wagner's ID photo with relief. *"Come see me,"* Wagner texted. Alex had one priority now – to rescue Ved and Sonia from Wagner. There would be time to grieve later, he thought. He had to keep his focus.

Getting back his flash drive back from Anne would save him a lot of time. He wouldn't have to regenerate code he had already written. That was a good thing.

Alex didn't think that Wagner would hurt Ved or Sonia. If Wagner wanted to hurt any of them, he could have done that at the park. He hoped that wasn't a rationalization. He hoped that it had been okay to take the time to take care of his mother and see her off.

Alex took out his phone and sent a text. *"What do you want?"* he asked Wagner, although he knew the answer. He wanted leverage.

He was alone, just like Anne had said. He felt immobilized, unable to stand or move his feet forward, but inertia put Ved and Sonia at greater risk, so he must ignore it.

His phone pinged. Alex took it out of his pocket and looked. *"Come to me,"* it said.

Yeah, I'll come see your pompous ass, Alex thought. As soon as I'm ready.

The light had shifted in Ved's office windows. Alex and Anne had worked for several hours before Alex gave up to stare out the window. When they heard footsteps coming down the hall, Anne's head snapped toward the door. She put her hand on her stun gun.

Frank stormed in.

Alex jumped toward the bookshelves and took a protective stance. Frank's eyes fell on the cardboard box on a shelf. "Is that my wife?"

Alex and Anne responded at the same time. "Ex-wife."

After a moment of silence, Alex exploded. He shouted, "Get out. I don't want you here." He physically pushed Frank toward the door.

"I've been looking for you."

"I don't care. I want you out."

Anne interjected herself between Frank and Alex. She attempted to push them apart. "Go to your corners," she commanded. She used all her strength to pull Alex into one corner. She pointed at him. "Stay or I'll handcuff you."

Alex lunged back toward Frank, but Anne pulled him back. In a minute, Alex was handcuffed to a desk chair in the corner. Frank slid into the easy chair in the opposite corner of the room. Anne circled in the middle, her arms outstretched, wary. She pointed to Alex.

"You," she said. "What's your problem?"

"He killed my mother."

"How can you say that?" Frank responded. "I loved your mother."

"Oh yeah. That's why you left her to die in a stinking pool of vomit while you lived it up inside the dome."

"Your mother and I divorced. I didn't know what would happen."

"You left us. You just shut down and hid. Like you always do." Alex sprang toward Frank, chair and all.

Anne jabbed him with her finger. "Back to your corner." She held up the power cord off an old lamp. "Or I'll make sure you do."

"Etta didn't want to live in the dome," Frank said. "She wanted to stay in our house so you could go to your school and hang out with your friends."

"You're blaming her?"

"Of course not. That's just how it was. No one knew how long the drought would last.

Alex shook his handcuffs.

"I didn't want you to be hungry. I set up a special account just for the two of you. Sam, the grocer who runs the neighborhood kiosk, was supposed to bring the food to you. It wasn't strictly legal..."

"Na-uh. You did not," Alex interrupted, lower lip out like a pouty child.

"Actually," Anne said. "He did. Charlie took over the account and used it to start the Black Market." She pinned Alex in his chair and stared into his eyes. "For a while I thought it was you." She looked for the truth. "The black market gouges starving people by charging triple food value or more." She found what she expected. Innocence. "Now I don't think you did that. You have too little, paid too much of a price, to believe that."

"How could someone do that?" Frank asked.

"The question is how could anyone do that?"

"Same way as you," Anne still watched Alex closely. "By accessing the data and making tiny changes with big impacts, the account number and the percent to distribute." She looked at Frank. "He goes in behind you and changes the database, thereby sending a good portion of the city's food supply to himself."

"Oh God. Who?" Frank asked.

"I don't know for sure, but you can bet he works for Wagner. That sort of operation couldn't go undetected without Wagner's approval."

"I can't believe it," Frank said, the full impact of this new knowledge weighing him down. "I sent food every week. I never forgot. I sent food."

Anne stood over Alex. He took a couple deep breaths. He looked still and calm. "Are we good?" she asked.

Alex nodded, so she removed the cuffs.

He ambled over to his messenger bag, toying with his computer in a suspicious way. Suddenly, Alex jumped out the window and rolled across the lawn. Anne or Frank barely had time to blink.

"See," Frank said. "It's easy to run away."

Chapter 33

Anne struck a match and put fire to a citronella candle on a little table between the two Adirondack chairs on the Harvey back porch. The candle created a soft circle of light. She stared across the flame to Frank who sat on one of his backyard chairs, his legs curled into his chest. He was making himself as small and protected as he could, his arms clutching his knees to his chest.

"Put out the light," Frank whispered. "If Alex knows that I'm here, he won't come home."

"You think Alex doesn't know you're here," Anne responded. "As long as you're squatting at his house, he'll never come here. You've essentially made him homeless."

Anne held the candle to Frank's face. The soft glow highlighted cuts and purpling bruises from his encounter with the mob at the gate.

"Dome security put you in jail," she said, "on the inside. How'd you get out?"

"They never keep anybody for long."

"I mean how did you get out of the dome?"

"Power's down." Frank went silent for a minute. "I should have built a pergola over the garden," he said, obviously thinking that said it all. "It's easy to convince yourself of anything if you want to believe badly enough. I convinced myself Alex and Etta were fine. They had the food I sent to the kiosk. They had the garden. But the food never arrived and the garden burned up. It would have been fine, if I'd built a pergola, like the porch, to diffuse the light. I never understood how badly I failed my family. No wonder Alex hates me."

"He hates you. That's a good thing," Anne said. "Hate is a strong emotion, the converse of love. It's when he doesn't care at all that you must worry."

Frank nodded toward a crumbling structure. "See the water reclamation tower? I built that when Alex was about two. There's a filter at the top of the tower. It gets clogged with twigs and leaves. Alex had to only see me climb the ladder once before he was scampering up like a little monkey to clean out the filter."

"He wants you to tell him you're sorry so he can forgive you."

Frank looked awful. "How far did Alex go? Did he knock me off the network?"

"He invaded the data in the Repository in order to zero out your accounts. I think it was so you would have as little as he and his mother. He wanted you to notice them."

Frank looked so desolate that Anne didn't know what to say next. "Alex. He'll come around," she tried.

"Why would he?" Frank said. "Etta was sick, starving. I won't forgive me." He uncurled and leaned forward toward Anne, creating an intimate scene around the dim light. "All I wanted was to save her, to save my family, to save all of us. I wanted to grow as much food as possible and share it with everyone."

"What happened?" Anne asked in a voice as soft as his.

"I didn't know anything had happened until you told me so."

"What's it like, living inside now?"

"We carry on because every day the Jumbotron in front of the Wagner Building tells us that we are making 'food for all.' We sacrifice for the happy, healthy images displayed of people on the outside."

Anne placed a hand on his knee to offer him some small comfort.

"There are bugs, big roaches that fly at your face, and rats, and little, tiny ants you can't get rid of."

Anne had seen signs of this when she lived in the dome. No surprise. The dome was a warm, wet spot that held the majority of the food supply.

Frank went on. "People grew bored, lonely, anxious, panicky, frantic, so Wagner added a sedative to the dome air to make the people docile. The only place you can get a clear head is inside the Wagner office building where people work. Designer cans of fresh air are distributed like illegal drugs. There's quite a market."

Frank was quiet for a while as Anne took all this in. "Wagner and, whew, Broadnack, they're fat, but even they couldn't eat all the food we've distributed. Where do you think the food has gone?"

Anne hesitated for a moment then answered him. "I think Wagner trades it for niceties that he and his inner circle desire."

"But, from where? There are no more niceties."

"Shreveport."

"But how can he get beyond the arid to get, well, anywhere? No one can pack enough water to make it that far and an electric car runs out of juice too quickly." Frank looked astonished for a moment. "Do they have gas?"

"No," Anne said. "They have camels."

"I'm sorry. Did you say camels?"

"Yes."

"But where did they get camels?" asked Frank.

"In Kerrville. There used to be an exotic animal ranch. They raised camels."

Frank stared at her in disbelief.

"If you hike along the train track to the left about sixteen miles beyond the split, there's a barn where a dozen camels are housed. Camels carry lots of heavy weight in climates too dry for horses or mules, and they can go long distances on little food and water. Camels make perfect sense."

Frank's brow was squashed in thought. "I was thinking, if Alex would leave…"

"There's nowhere else to go," she interrupted. "The wet sounds worse. Harder to survive. We have water and electricity. We grow food. We make do," Anne said. "Some people even think we're in recovery. Besides," Anne went on. "Alex would never leave. Alex takes care of the people he loves. That's just what he does. If you don't know that, you don't know Alex at all." That came out sounding harsher than she intended, but Frank didn't seem to notice.

"Who does Alex love?" he asked.

Anne gentled her voice. "He loves a pretty, red-haired girl named Sonia and her grandfather."

"You seem to know Alex pretty well. How long have you known him?"

"I just met Alex in person today, but I've been watching him via security cameras for months."

"What's Alex done to deserve such high scrutiny?"

"Alex is the only person outside the dome, maybe the only person anywhere, who can safely hack into the Repository and change the code."

"Why is that? I know that so many of the people with critical skills died, but it seems that coding would be given high priority to relearn."

"We've been working on that, but with any code that was built by this one man, which is most of the critical code, has traps we can't get beyond."

"Kolli Vedkka? That's how Alex got beyond the traps. He had help."

"What do you mean," Anne asked.

Frank looked surprised. "Ved Poutin is Kolli Vedkka. You didn't know that?"

"It crossed my mind."

"So, Alex has the ultimate control. Wagner thinks he's become the ultimate threat. Wagner took Sonia and Ved captive to control Alex," Frank deduced.

"Ironically, Wagner set up the showdown with Alex that he most feared. Alex will do whatever it takes to get them back. Including tearing it all down."

"So what's he planning to do?"

"He can't do anything until we figure out where Pierce is keeping Sonia and Ved. We know they're inside the dome, but where?"

"And that's what Alex needs right now. To find out where Sonia and Ved are being held?"

Anne nodded.

"Do you have a photo of them?" Frank asked.

"I can get one."

"How can I get in touch once I find them?"

"What are you thinking?"

He didn't answer.

She pulled a stun gun off her belt. "Take this. I can get another."

"But, weapons are illegal for citizens."

Anne gave Frank an incredulous look. "You don't think you'll have to break a few laws?"

Frank took the gun. "I'll leave in the morning."

Nancy Smith

Part III

Chapter 34

Frank didn't want to go back inside the dome. His safe haven was neither safe nor a haven any longer. He paced for a minute, agitated and miserable, but then he started to pack.

He found a small duffle that was just where he left it in the hallway closet, but his toolbox in the garage was a wreck with half of it missing. He threw a hammer, wire cutters and an old rusty screwdriver with a rubber handle into the bag. In the kitchen, he added sunscreen and a large bottle of water.

He picked up Anne's little gift. It felt large and heavy in his hand. He wrapped the stun gun in plastic and threw it in the duffle. He searched Etta's grandfather's desk for money and came up with seventy-eight cents in change. How long had it been since he'd needed cash? Any additional space in the duffle he filled with food. Thinking that they might be his last meal, he took some crackers in a little plastic bin, two cans of soup and a peach. The irony of stealing food from his son did not escape him.

He pulled on a ball cap, laced up some heavy boots and left the house in the gray dawn, just before the sun peaked over the horizon. He walked to the train station and caught the Number One train to the dome.

Out the window of the train, Frank watched the red glow of a simmering fire. Sunrise burst on the horizon looking like a terrain from Hell. It occurred to him that the fires might have been set intentionally to ensure that the public didn't venture too near the camel stables or the food trains that Wagner loaded in the desert.

Frank got off the train in an abandoned area two stops shy of the dome. A concrete curb lined the unfinished pavement with half-completed, half-destroyed home construction. He cautiously looked around. He spotted the river with the dome in the distance. Between him and the dome was about five miles of rock-hard, barren dirt, deeply cracked from lack of water. There were filth and decay, but no people.

He stepped slowly, gingerly, paying close attention to where he placed his feet. The dirt began to slither. He saw several triangle-shaped heads attached to coils half-buried in the dirt. Rattlesnakes. The venomous snakes blended with the ground.

After he could breathe again, Frank gave the snakes a wide berth. He took one quiet stride, waited, then another. He heard the famous jangle before he saw a diamond shaped pattern slide across his path. The viper head lifted and exposed his fangs, but did not strike. Frank waited for the snake to pass. He took another careful step. The sun rose in the sky at a pace that matched his slow progress.

By midday, Frank had made it to the river. He pulled his water bottle from the duffle and took a long gulp, letting a few drops slip down his chin. He ate one of his crackers and then stashed the rest in his duffle.

As he walked around, he spotted a plywood board roughly five feet by three feet that looked perfect. Focused on the board, he didn't see the tree branch before it connected with the back of his head. Everything went black.

Frank woke alone by the side of the river. His fingers found the bump on the crown of his head. He stroked his burned nose and forehead and gingerly touched the blisters on his face. They felt like about fifteen or twenty minutes in the sun.

Frank spent another hour searching for the person who hit him. He needed his tools. He didn't find the vagrant, but he did find the duffle. It was in a dugout made of rocks and branches that housed a torn and dirty blanket and a tin camp cup. The crackers were gone, as were his ball cap and sunscreen, but the rest of his stuff was still in his bag.

In the distance, he saw a stick-thin homeless man running toward him screaming like a banshee. Frank slung the duffle over his shoulder and ran for the river. He picked up his plywood board and threw it into the water. He paddled toward the distant shore. The water didn't stop the hungry man. He would drown before he even slowed down. Frank pulled a can of soup from his duffel. He showed the can to the hungry man and threw it to the nearest shore. Frank breathed with relief when the hungry man turned around and went for the food, not him. A can on the shore was worth more than two in the water.

Frank paddled with his hands across the narrowest part of the river toward the basin at the base of the dam. As he got closer, he jumped in, clothes, boots, duffel and all. In the water, he pushed the board away from him. Frank watched it float in the direction of the opposite shore and the hungry man. He swam to the basin's shore.

Frank climbed fifty feet up the retaining wall beside the dam to the reservoir. He rubbed his hands raw as he ascended over loose boulders. He stood on the cement ledge that surrounded the powerhouse for the turbines. Early evening air chilled his wet skin, making him shiver.

Frank faced a heavy two-layer titanium door. From the other direction, he had simply walked out, leaving the door to swing shut behind him. If the power had been on, Frank's thumbprint would have opened the locking bolts on the door to the powerhouse, but the power was off. He wasn't certain what would happen when he tried the outside entrance.

Of course, it didn't open. He kicked the door a few times with his heavy boots. Nothing. He pulled the hammer from the duffle and pounded the doorknob until it fell off. He kicked the door again until the bolt bent and gave way.

Frank stepped into the cool, dark powerhouse and breathed a sigh of relief. It was quiet, the mammoth turbines under his feet still. He crossed a gangplank and opened the door for the service shaft that rose 160 feet up the side of the dam.

As he climbed the service shaft, Frank could almost feel the weight of all the water in the reservoir pushing against the dam. It was cold and black with zero visibility in the tunnel. He put a foot on the next rung up until he reached the top.

Water was a poor conductor of electricity. It's the dirt in the water that makes water and electricity a dangerous mix. Just two days before, the grate had been sparking, but he now bet his life that, like the day before, it now was not. Wagner had a generator they were likely working to bring online, but he knew it only powered the most vital functions. This entry gate for the dam that he had so easily pushed to open to leave the day before was not at the top of anyone's list. It may not have been on a list at all.

Frank dug the insulated screwdriver from a zippered pocket of his duffle. He held the screwdriver on its rubber end and pointed it toward the iron mesh of the gate. He sucked in his breath and waited. No electrical arc. He touched the mesh tentatively, waiting to fry like a fish in a pan of oil. Nothing happened. He was still alive. Frank cut the mesh with his wire cutters and slipped through the hole.

There was a guard on the dam. Frank had a stun gun, but was too far away to use it. The guard spotted him and ran toward Frank, so Frank did a swan dive from the top of the dam into the interior lake. Frank surfaced and looked back.

The guard didn't follow, fear clouding his eyes, and it came to Frank. He couldn't swim. He was young, likely hadn't grown up with as much water around as was in the lake. Where would he learn to swim?

Chapter 35

Frank was inside the dome. In the water. In the lake. He ducked under and swam toward shore. When he surfaced, he could see Cy inside his houseboat pacing from window to window to door.

Cy spotted him, focused on him and then came outside. Cy could always be depended on to act in the most appalling way possible. He ran down the pier, yelling to the guard at the far side of the dome. "Breach."

A roving beach patrol heard him, but looked confused.

"That's Franklin Harvey. He's wanted by Wagner. He escaped. I saw it on the news. He's breached dome defenses," Cy filled in. "Look. He's swimming with his clothes on."

Frank ducked under again and swam for as long as he could, but ultimately he needed air.

The security guard saw him and spoke via a walkie-talkie with another guard on the dam.

Cy hopped onto a jetski and sped across the lake. He raised a wake as he turned the jet aiming for Frank's head. Frank had to dive under the water to save himself. When he surfaced, he was dangerously close to Cy.

"This isn't necessary," Frank yelled. "I'm coming in."

Frank swam toward the shore with the expertise of a man who had swum every day. Cy came after Frank with a fierceness that Frank didn't understand. He and Cy played an impressive game of keep away.

A couple of Wagner's security guards on a small speedboat joined Cy. They pulled Frank into the boat and docked it. The guards seemed uncommitted. They didn't even hold his arm as they scrambled onto the deck. Frank wondered if they might let him go. He didn't want that.

"I give up," he called. "Take me to jail."

Frank wanted to see if Ved and Sonia were being held in the cells. He came quietly.

The guards prep walked him down the pier and into the jailhouse. They threw him into one of four small cells, all that had ever really been needed in the dome. Frank checked each cell as they walked by. All empty. Frank didn't really think Ved and Sonia would be there, but he had to check. If Wagner had something to hide, Frank knew where it would be.

Chapter 36

From the roof of the train station, Alex watched through the transparent dome as Frank was pulled from the lake and arrested. Alex slid down the pole supporting the deck cover and headed directly for the edge of the biodome.

With quiet stealth, Alex climbed the infrastructure of the dome. Like a monkey, he jumped from grid to grid. In short time, he was on the opposite side. He swung his body to the ledge of the dam and through the still-unlocked gate. He slid directly into the water, never making a splash.

Alex gasped and struggled with his buoyancy. This was a first for Alex. Never in his memory had he been completely submerged in wet. He did a terrifying, death-defying dogpaddle from one support pole under the pier to the next. He gasped for breath as he scrambled gratefully ashore. From his first step at the train station to his first step on shore to Dad's houseboat, it was twenty minutes flat.

Alex could see Cy in his kitchen, so he slithered to the opposite side of Frank's boat. He balanced on a narrow shelf of deck, took off his shirt and wrapped it around his hand. He pushed the shatterproof glass on the bedroom window until it broke loose and fell inside. He slipped through the window and closed the heavy blinds.

He watched Cy. Cy heard the noise. He stood, looked around, but saw nothing amiss.

Alex entered the kitchen. He found a candle, lit it and carried it into the back. He took a shower and put on some of Frank's dry clothes.

Back in the kitchen, he searched for food, but there was not much. He found Frank's duffle with a can of soup. As he ate it cold, Alex vowed to slip into the hydroponics farm the next day and steal a bag full or two.

In the living room, Alex searched the top drawer of Frank's desk. He found a notebook with curled corners, a stash of colored pencils of all lengths and sharpness, a manual pencil sharpener, a dozen paperclips and some duct tape. Alex also found Frank's ID card and hung it around his neck.

Alex pulled out the drawing pad and opened it. There were sketches of him and his Mom; him playing on the monkey bars in the park; him nestled in Mom's arms; Mom flying through the train station – the only color the red of her dress; and him, standing outside the dome, an angry scowl on his eight-year-old face, his hands on his hips. Alex felt touched and disturbed by the drawings.

Before Alex decided how he felt about it, Frank stepped through the front door.

"Son," Frank said.

Alex said nothing.

"The old man and the pretty girl aren't in the dome jail."

"They let you out?" Alex asked.

"Where am I going to go? I'm supposed to report to Wagner in the morning for a little chat."

"Have you any idea where Wagner might keep them?"

"Yeah, I know," Frank said. "I know where he keeps all his hidden things." He peered into the empty soup can. He looked like he wanted to say something, but couldn't.

Chapter 37

It was surprisingly easy for Alex to walk into the Power Station. With the power down, there was no thumbprint authorization, no identification numbers, no voice recognition or heartbeat monitoring. Alex kept his cap low as he flashed Frank's ID card at the guard station. The conductive ink on the ID card called up no database. There wasn't even a photo of Frank.

"Purpose?" the guard asked.

"I'm here to fix the main computer." It was unlikely the guard would ask why a botanist was messing with the super computer. There was no access to any database to determine Frank's occupation.

"Won't do much good. It's a black hole in there. Generator's not up an' runnin' yet."

"You know when that might be?" Alex asked.

"Don't you know?" the guard answered.

"I won't need the generator if I can get the power station operational again."

The guard looked skeptical. "You can do that?" He didn't wait for a response. "You can't be alone with the computers. I'll have to stick."

Alex nodded.

The guard stuck out his hand. "Lt. Boris Foma," he said.

Alex shook his hand. "Frank Harvey," Alex replied.

Another guard stood in for Boris at the guard's station while he showed Alex to the computer room. Boris led him down a dim corridor illuminated by Boris' flashlight and a skylight many stories up. Alex paid close attention to his surroundings as the guard escorted him through the facility. The hall was narrow and lined in steel panels. It felt close, metallic, like the inside of a submarine, or, at least what he thought a submarine would be like. Deep in the center of the power station, a vertical support reached all the way to the top of the dome. Alex looked up.

"Hey Boris," he said. "Is that open up there?"

"That's the tower for the heliostat mirrors."

Boris unlocked a tiny room and let Alex in. The room was a void with absolutely no light. "I don't have an extra flashlight," Boris said.

Alex set up his laptop and turned it on. "I have light," he informed the guard. Boris looked quizzical. Then the soft glow of the monitor lit Alex's face.

In the last couple of days, he and Anne had spent many hours walled up in Ved's office talking about community versus isolation, inclusion versus exclusion and unfortunate death versus murder.

"If I'd known the consequences," Alex had said, "I'd never have messed with the Repository."

Anne had interrupted him. "You're too hard on yourself. You didn't do this." Anne said.

Alex asked, "Who did?"

"I think one of my officers. Zach Garland. He's been messing around in computer systems where he ought not be. He's competent, but also arrogant and fearless. He wouldn't care about consequences."

Alex had used his unique skills to annoy and torment his father. He'd hit traps, but had made it his responsibility to fix them. Where he had trouble, Ved had been there to help. But now, he wasn't. Alex was on his own.

Alex thought Anne was emotionally worn out by death. She saw it every day and not just on the death carts. And, she had her own trauma to deal with. Alex remembered the horror of seeing her husband die as only a child could. Many people had insulated themselves, but Alex doubted she could do that, even if she wished to. She wanted things to get better, actually be better. Friends wanted to be reunited with friends. Families split apart wanted to be together — other people's families, of course.

He wanted to go beyond survival or wanting revenge to thinking about, fighting for, what was best for everyone. The plan he and Anne developed was modest. He would restore the power grid so people would have electricity and then dismantle the gate's security so the community was forced to unite. While he did that, Anne would shut down the black market and take back the food that had been plundered. Then, there might truly be food for all. That meant that Frank was the only person left who didn't have a job and could find and free Ved and Sonia. That scared him the most.

Chapter 38

Standing in Wagner's public office with its clandestine extension behind its secret door, Frank didn't feel like a member of the Wagner team any longer.

"Harvey?" Wagner looked annoyed. "You look terrible." Wagner noshed on a breakfast taco. Frank's mouth watered and his stomach gurgled. He felt faint. He'd only had two fingers of Nutella, three bites of sandwich and a cracker in more than forty-eight hours.

Frank had suffered from dehydration and fever once when he was a child. From that experience, he knew the next step was to no longer be able to hold down food at all. He'd get weak and worthless. How long did that take? The vomiting. Like Etta. His Etta.

There was an empty plate of crumbs with a garnish of grapes. Frank took them and ate them.

"I don't know if you've been told," Frank said, "but, my ex-wife passed away."

"Sorry for your loss." Wagner's voice dripped with insincerity. He didn't care.

"Thanks," Frank choked out.

"So, your son is alone on the outside. What's your plan?"

"I've been thinking about bringing him in."

"From what I understand your son is very self-reliant and not much of a fan of the Wagner Company. I doubt he would come inside willingly."

"You're probably right about that." Frank was miffed. Wagner knew all about his situation and had already made up his mind.

"You've been a loyal employee and have done a good job, so I'll do you this favor and tell you, if your son comes into this dome, I'll arrest him."

Frank felt a surge of heat. "He's my son. He's a child. He's alone out there. He's just lost his mother." Frank struggled to regain his calm. It didn't matter that he knew Alex was okay and already inside the dome. Frank needed to focus and keep his cool.

"We'd hate to lose a man of your inventiveness and talent. Any way to work this out?"

"Not without Alex."

"Then, maybe you should go out to be with your son," Wagner said.

Frank decided that this was his punishment for his erratic behavior of late. He was being shut out. After everything that Frank had done for Wagner, he was dumbfounded. "You don't have to kick me out. I'll leave, but there's something I need to do for my son first."

"What's that?" Wagner asked.

Frank pulled the stun gun from his jacket pocket and sent a jolt of current into Wagner's chest. He held the charge longer than was necessary. Wagner hit the floor like a rock. He spasmed and then laid still. Frank kicked him hard enough in the ribs to leave a bruise. That's what it felt like being down.

Frank finished Wagner's taco, ate a handful of nuts he found at the bar while he searched for the barely hidden latch that opened the only slightly better hidden bookcase door. He pulled Wagner out of sight.

Chapter 39

The computer room was located in the powerstation. The guard, Boris, was getting nervous. He fidgeted, picking up items on the desk and putting them back down. Alex wasn't taken in by the purposefully bland, bored expression on his face.

"Will you stop that? It's distracting." Alex keyed fast.

"How much longer?"

"Not sure."

Alex looked at the guard. "Would you consider getting me a cup of coffee? I need caffeine." Boris hesitated. "It'll go faster," Alex urged.

Anne and Alex's attack on Wagner was flawed only in that it demanded that Alex trust his father with the most important part to him. Anne would get the pilfered food and bring it back to the starving people outside the dome. Alex would power up the electric infrastructure and disable the security at the gate. But Frank?

Anne assured Alex that with the power down and all the commotion the two of them would create that Frank's task would be easy enough. She said that there was only that funky four-cell jail, maybe one or two guards on it. Already that had gone awry.

Boris pulled out a walkie-talkie. Alex didn't realize he had that.

"Need backup at the computer room. I'm taking a little stroll."

As they walked down the hallway, the motion detecting lights came on. The generator was on. Alex had hoped that the computer room was on a generator. He must be right.

At the computer room, the guard opened the door. Thankfully, Boris stepped out of the room. In a minute, Alex could hear the two guards whispering outside the door. The backup guard, a big, brute of a man, seemed paranoid. Alex couldn't hear what Boris was saying, but he could hear the tone of the brute's response.

Brutus said, "When he's done, we should detain him. I don't know what he's doing in there. Do you?"

Boris' response was a garble.

In the dim light of the computer room, Alex keyed to save his life. They were likely saving generator power for the most important things. Online, he argued with some semi-skilled programmer in some other room somewhere within the dome's intranet who thought he was smarter than Alex, but he was not. Bright lights flashed and blinked as the dome's main computer hummed on. Alex sighed. Light. Noise. It felt like ...relief. The power station was back up.

Alex plugged his laptop computer into the dome's main terminal. He sent a file with an Easter egg, a hidden character you had to know was there to find. It brought up a picture of the Bastille in France with the caption "Storm the Bastille." This Easter egg would call people to the gate, to the train station, to the position where Anne would bring the food.

Despite the happy irony of sending the call to arms from deep within the bowels of the dome, inside the power station, inside the computer room, that wasn't what Alex was here to do and he had only a few minutes left to do it. He attached the flash drive and started a massive copy of new computer code designed to dismantle the locks at the gateway and strip the power from the infrastructure of the dome. He'd added his own firewalls and traps, so it was unlikely anyone could easily undo his work.

Chapter 40

When the network was restored, Anne watched Frank and Alex jabber at each other on their Nomads. She couldn't get them to talk to each other. It was exhausting. They were orchestrating a revolution, and she had to act as go-between for two petulant boys, only one of which was actually a teen.

Anne and a dozen of her most trusted, handpicked officers tramped through the desert. All she had told them was that they were on a secret mission that would change their lives. She hoped that most, if not all, would think the change was for the better.

They were heavily armed. The officers had to wonder about that as they marched, laden with whatever weapons she could find, through a no-man's land that was supposed to be impassable and uninhabitable. What they knew about were snakes and fires and unyielding heat. What they didn't know about made them fearful and silent, each dealing with their angst in their own fashion.

They had started in a van from the north side of town at about three o'clock in the morning. The officers were probably wondering about that too. They picked up the train tracks about three miles out, beyond eyesight from the dome, even with a zoom lens. They followed the tracks another two miles, and then they left the van behind and began plodding across the wasteland.

In the distance, she could see them now. The camel stables. The officers saw them too and shuffled restlessly. It was a tall and long stone structure, with six arched doors about twelve feet in height. Windows surrounded the top of the building, carved out of the last foot of stone before the roof.

"What's in there?" Officer June asked.

"Camels."

"Camels?"

"They use them to steal our food and sell it to Shreveport. No telling how much of our food is being shipped out. Food we need."

The officers muttered and shuffled, holding back a barely suppressed rage. Everyone had lost someone to starvation.

"What are we going to do?" June asked.

"Here's the plan. We are one of three teams working simultaneously. One team is going to restore the power station and bring down the gate at the dome. One team is rescuing trapped prisoners, including an important scientist." She could see she had them. They were with her and would do anything she asked. "And, we're going to put an end to the theft of our food," said Anne.

From a lonely hut at the far end, a solitary man exited with a snow shovel. Since it was unlikely to snow in the desert, Anne took the shovel as an indicator of the size of his mucking out job. She watched for a few minutes, but didn't see any other people.

The solitary man spotted Anne, glared at her as a train approached along the rail tracks from town. The man returned to his house and came out with something that may have been a gun, but there was something odd about it. She couldn't tell from this distance. He shot a red flare into the sky. The red light trailed sparks as it fell to earth. Oh, she thought.

"Pick up your pace," she snapped. At their current rate they would barely make the station before the train did.

The troop double-timed to the stables. Anne took the flare gun from the man and gently escorted the man back into his hut, talking to him soothingly all the time.

"What's your name?" she asked.

He stuck out his lower lip and chin in a belligerent manner.

"No name. Okay." She glanced at the snow shovel leaning against the wall in the corner. "For now, I'll call you Chuck." Yeah, Chuck with the giant muck.

She handcuffed Chuck to a scuffed iron bedframe and taped his mouth. She and two officers did a quick search of the area for soldiers and weapons before the train arrived. There were none. Anne had the officers conceal themselves in the cabin and the stables. She watched out a dust-covered window.

The train pulled to a stop as the sky turned gray with dawn light. Officer Garland stepped off the final car out into the fading darkness. He glanced toward the cabin, scanned the area and then nodded.

Four men followed him onto the platform. Anne and her group of twelve remained hidden behind the tall wall of the camel barn. They watched as Garland's team led out the camels and quickly packed the groceries from the train on the animal's backs.

"Not that one," Garland said.

When he was ready to send the camels on their way, Anne noted that a dozen boxes of food remained on the train's loading dock.

Garland was the person stealing food. It all fell into place for her. Garland bought the FFEA account from Charlie Broadnack. He modified the amounts and locations – not too risky – to send food to himself. But where? Mixed in the secret shipment to Shreveport. Where else?

Garland was part of a small team who were tasked with trying to learn the computer code. Anne thought he was dedicated and enthusiastic. He must have gotten cocky. It would be just like him to do something beyond his expertise and ability. He did something to the original code, despite all her warnings. He had set off the blackout.

The camels huffed and pawed the ground as Anne moved in. "Interesting." She peeked into the topmost box. Peaches. "These Aren't going too far. Back to town? This helps prove the black market case. I bet Pierce will be happy to hear about this?"

"Well Detective Roget, this is a surprise," Garland said.

"Not so much for me," Anne replied.

Garland glanced around and did a head count – twelve officers to his four thieves. Three of the officers, including Officer June, flanked Garland. "Who are we arresting?" he asked as if he just happened to be there, as if he were on the job.

Anne walked close to Garland. June handed Anne a set of handcuffs.

"You," she said.

Chapter 41

Frank dragged Wagner through the secret door in the bookshelf and stood in the largest living space he had seen in a decade. The room was round with a door every five feet, like a wagon wheel. It felt like being in a funhouse. Frank picked a door. What's behind door number one?

Voila. It was a bedroom with a messy, unmade four-poster bed that looked like it just came off the plantation. All the furniture was heavy, dark, old wood and covered in unwashed clothes. Frank dragged Wagner to the far side of the bed, tied him with the cord of a bedside lamp, stuffed his mouth with a ripped pillowcase and left him there. He went back to the living room.

Door two was a storage room filled with an odd assortment of what looked like memorabilia: oil paintings, art glass, and bone china. Frank paused for a minute at a pair of ornate finials probably made for the roof of a house. He tried to lift one thinking he could make his duffle into a weapon, but it was too heavy. He put the finial back on the shelf next to a box of Christmas ornaments.

Door number three led to a hall and two more solid-core doors. Behind one, Frank heard wheezing and gasping for breath. Someone inside the room heard him and slapped at the door.

"Help! He needs help!" Frank heard a sweet, high voice.

"Sonia?"

"Yes."

Frank futilely banged on the door with one hand as he jiggled the doorknob with the other. Using the screwdriver from his bag, Frank banged off the hinges of the door and pulled it from its frame. Inside, the old man gasped for breath. The red-haired girl looked worried as she held his hand and spoke to him in a calming voice.

"Alex sent me." Frank took one side of Ved and Sonia took the other. Ved could barely walk, so they made slow progress down the hall.

Under his breath, Frank prayed. *Don't die. Don't die.* How could he face Alex again if he couldn't bring back his mentor and his girlfriend – both intact?

The last door opened to a garage at the back of the dome that also served as the loading ramp for the train. Frank knew there must be one from the way that Anne described the loading of food boxes she had seen from her balcony.

The garage held three vehicles: an electric car, a golf cart and a gas car. Though he didn't know the make, he could tell it was nice car by the style and lines. Spaces were designated for each of the cars on the concrete floor. The walls were covered in a shelving system made of iron piping. An overhead door filled one wall across a vast open space. The door was open.

Ved's coughing turned into a wheeze and then a painful struggle to breathe. As Frank lowered him to the cement floor, Ved grasped the tightness in his chest.

"He needs his respirator," Sonia said.

Frantically, Frank examined the oversized car, a Lincoln Escalade it said on the body. He put Ved in the back where he'd be comfortable as Frank drove to Etta's hospital. He figured it'd take about twenty minutes. Frank opened the driver's side door and settled in behind the wheel. Sonia crawled in the back of the car with her grandfather.

He couldn't remember the last time he drove. It wasn't that long after he'd gotten his driver's license. He pushed the start button, but nothing happened. He remembered something about the brake pedal and jabbed at it again. Nothing. He tried the electric car, but it was also dead and wouldn't start. The golf cart had no battery.

Frank noted Ved's skin was taking on a pale, bluish tone. He needed air. Here Frank was again, making a choice that could mean life or death for someone that Alex loved.

"I have some oxygen on my houseboat," he said. "Let's go."

Chapter 42

On the train platform, Garland looked at the handcuffs in Anne's hands and laughed. He was still trying to use his charm to get out of his obvious criminal activities—even as the stolen food surrounded him. Anne smiled, too, incredulous at his gall—until, over his shoulder, an army rose up, barreling toward them in clouds of dust. They were on motorcycles, dozens of men with assault weapons about a quarter mile away.

The flare, she thought—damn it, damn it. They must be responding to the flare.

As Anne opened her mouth to warn the others, Garland head-butted her, knocking the wind out of her and sending her staggering backward. When she looked up, gasping, he had grabbed June and dragged her a few steps away, holding a knife to her throat.

The rider who was closest to Anne, a New Age cowboy, slung his gun up ready to open fire.

Garland clocked June a good blow in the ribs, hard enough to break. He pulled himself up onto the nearest camel, but June hung on to his leg.

"Let go," Anne yelled, but June didn't.

The motorcycles were on them. The riders opened with a hail of bullets. Anne fell to the protection of the ground, keeping her head low. Gradually, the riders quit shooting, as if confused by the situation. Who was the enemy? Anne was confused as well. She didn't know these men who were dressed in a uniform she didn't recognize. Who were they?

Garland used his boot to smash June's face again and again. He propelled the camel to run and the camel took off. Anne was stunned at how fast the animal moved.

"Let go," Anne yelled again.

Garland's actions made him look guilty so some of the cowboys chased him. Surprisingly, the camel was giving the riders a good run.

June hung on with her left arm as she clawed for purchase with her right hand. Her nails dug into Garland's arm. He kicked her viciously in the mouth until blood flowed. She tumbled through the camels pounding legs and lay in a heap in the dust.

Garland escaped on his camel. He was gone. "For now," Anne said.

Anne slapped the remaining camels on the butt. She flailed her arms, hoping that the cowboys would chase the food. Some did, but not all, so she laid down cover fire as she ran to the mangled arms and legs that were June. Anne threw June's crumpled body over her shoulder.

"Get on the train," she screamed to her crew.

Anne dumped June on the platform and pulled her into the nearest car. The engineer lunged at her, but she whirled out of his way. Her thick, wavy hair flowed as she spun.

"Get onto the train," she yelled again to her officers.

She flipped the engineer into the dirt on the side of the tracks, climbed into the engine car. She looked over the controls. Most were clearly marked. A two-year-old could drive this train. She put the it into reverse and set the speed to full. "Hold On," she screamed. The train barreled backward at breakneck speed. She hoped all her people had managed to grab on. One of her guys took over the controls.

"Stay low," she yelled. Bullets flew over their heads as they hugged the floor. The riders stayed with the train for about a mile and then fell behind.

It wasn't supposed to go like that. Anne rocked June in her arms. They were supposed to go in, tie up the two or three guards who were usually there, get the food and bring it back to the crowd at the dome. It had gone so terribly wrong.

Anne pulled a lock of hair out of the blood caking June's face. "You'll be okay," Anne lied. The other officers crowded around. They looked as if they thought it unlikely that June would be fine. Anne took June's slim hand with her partially painted fingernails and held it to her heart. She rocked June until the battered woman breathed her last breath.

Anne looked up. She counted twelve officers: three hurt and one dead. Her head wouldn't clear. She couldn't make a rational thought. She knew she was going into shock. She was feeling a little dizzy. She knew the first thing she must do. She sent a message to Alex.

"Blood spilled. Get out of there."

Chapter 43

In the computer room, Alex listened as Brutus, the paranoid guard, whispered to Boris outside the door. Brutus peered into the room and glared at Alex.

Alex's phone pinged. He saw the first word "blood."

"Trouble..." someone shouted from the walkie-talkie. "...need immediate help."

It was time to go. Brutus rushed at him as Alex tried to pass in the doorway, but Alex was able to knock the guard off balance.

"Oh God," said Boris.

As Alex fled the computer room, he saw Boris pull the cables that connected the two computers disrupting his program. His routine didn't finish. There was no telling how far it had gone.

Brutus was nearly on Alex, so Alex ran at the narrow submarine hallway wall and walked up it, one hand and foot on each wall. Alex jumped to the center pole and shimmied up. Brutus shimmied up the pole after Alex giving it his best effort, but he slipped back down into the corridor. He didn't make a quarter of the distance that Alex covered.

Alex fled out the ventilation hole at the top of the dome. Orange light bounced off the mirrors as Alex climbed outside. He heard the ruckus of the rioters on the ground before he saw them.

Through the transparent dome, Alex saw Boris bolt toward the locked gate. Boris looked up and spotted Alex as he began a slow and careful descent down the infrastructure.

A siren sounded. Damnation. Alex's plan was supposed to work in two phases. First, he restored the power and then he would initiate a new routine to shut down the security. But, he had to fly and Boris pulled the plug. The program didn't complete. It looked like the power was up, but the security wasn't down. The grid was coming up with full power.

The dome's security did not activate all at once. It turned on in sections. First the lights blinked red as a warning and then turned a steady white to indicate full power. The first section to activate was the gateway to outside. Boris pushed his way out of the dome and began his careful climb toward Alex.

Rioters saw this activity as a call to action. They swarmed the dome's surface. Security guards struggled to hold them back. Even so some rioters broke through the line and climbed up.

Alex watched as Boris moved dangerously close. Boris grabbed for Alex's foot in an attempt to pull him down to the curved surface.

"Hey Boris," Alex smiled.

"Hey Frank."

Alex shook free and jumped down one grid.

Boris pulled his baton.

The dome lights blinked red in the next section over from the gate.

Rioters in that section who had climbed the dome turned and scrambled to get back down. Almost as one, guards and rioters turned to assist the people's escape. All that was important was getting everyone out of harm's way. They formed a mosh pit that caught people as they jumped from the dome's surface.

Chapter 44

Frank tried to look casual as he and Sonia assisted Ved to Frank's houseboat. Cy was on his houseboat roof making a few repairs with a hammer and nails. Cy stopped his pounding to inspect the three of them.

"He okay?" Cy asked.

Frank gave Cy an angry glare.

"Who is that?"

"None of your business," Frank replied.

Frank heard the warning siren. Something had gone wrong. He searched the growing crowd outside the dome for signs of Alex.

Frank and his visitors slipped into his front door. He and Sonia laid Ved out on the living room sofa. As Sonia moved into the kitchen to get Ved a glass of water, Frank pulled the fresh air canister from its clasp under the sofa. He took a whiff before he affixed the mask to Ved. Sonia returned, lifted the mask a bit to give Ved a sip. She stroked his hair and mumbled softly to soothe her grandfather. Frank laid a light blanket over Ved's trembling body.

Frank heard yelling. He stepped out onto his sun deck to investigate the commotion. Movement in his peripheral vision caused him to look up. He saw Alex and Boris fighting above him on the outer surface of the dome.

As Cy climbed down the ladder at the side of his houseboat, Frank rushed him and grabbed Cy's hammer. Frank ran for the gate. He evaded the guards, themselves too occupied with the angry crowd, and forced himself against the tide. Frank jumped on the dome exterior and started up the dome's surface.

One of the rioters tried to hold Frank back. "My son," he shouted. Frank pointed and the rioter saw Alex struggling for the baton with Boris. The rioter let go of Frank.

Frank had trouble keeping his footing on the curved surface of the dome. He jumped the border of a grid just as the lights began to go white with flowing current.

Frank skittered on the sloped edge of the dome. He reached Alex and Boris as the lights turned white one section away. Frank swung the hammer and knocked Boris' feet from under him. Boris dropped his baton, but managed to retrieve it before Frank was steady on his feet again. Frank and Boris went at it, hammer to baton.

Alex lunged at Boris, who deftly moved out of his way, causing Alex to lose his balance in the process. Alex tumbled down the dome, grasping and missing a strut. Frank ran after him, letting the hammer fall away.

Boris was adroit for a big man. He got up, steady, regained his footing quickly. He made another run at Alex, as Alex slipped down the side of the curved surface.

Frank reached for Alex too. As the lights in their section turned red with a tingle of electricity soon to be fatal, Frank used his left arm to toss Alex off the dome into the waiting crowd below and then he leaped into the night.

All the biodome lights were steady white.

Chapter 45

Her officer managed to drive the train into the downtown depot. Anne called for a forensics team and a medical examiner. She put out a BOLO for Garland and sent his picture to every train station on the newly restored network. Anne stayed long enough to see June safe in the hands of the M.E.

Anne jumped a train for the dome station and she was buried deep in the crowd outside the dome when she heard the siren. She couldn't get through the packed protesters, so she pulled her Nomad. She called up the biodome camera. Her face turned glum as she focused on the images on her phone. She forced and pushed and ran toward the action.

Anne saw the bodies, falling through the sky from the dome's shell. Tears slid down her face. She screamed, primal and with remembered pain.

Chapter 46

Pierce Wagner lay on the floor of his own bedroom. His wrists were raw from struggling and his mouth was dry. He felt a pain in his side that could only mean a huge bruise. He'd been there for what felt like hours, left to his own thoughts.

Pierce's family had always had more money than God. His father had made a fortune on pharmaceuticals, government utilities and communications contracts. He and his cronies, the one percent who made all the wealth, bought up control over the representatives, senators, governors and even presidents. They owned the military and the police. They used their money to discredit science and journalism and the evidence of people's own eyes. They would do anything to protect their wealth, even as the human cry went up, even as they realized that they had ruined the earth and ruined the sky. Now Dad was dead and Pierce had more wealth than Dad.

As a kid, Pierce, his brother and his parents had lived in a mansion on the shores of Lake Travis. Three floors of finely furnished rooms – five bedrooms and seven baths, a screening room, a workout room, a library, two living spaces and two dining spaces off a generously-sized indoor kitchen. Outside, there had been two decks and an outdoor kitchen for just the four of them. There had also been a boathouse larger than most people's homes with a speedboat for water skiing and a sailboat.

His mother had died and then his brother. He had inherited this home from his father when he died and had chosen to live there himself as an adult. After her divorce, Pierce's daughter, Parker and her son moved in as well. Parker had died in the first pandemic and had left behind her little son.

And then his fine home was destroyed on two fronts. Hordes. First, hordes of insects: termites chipped at the wood framing, roaches filled the walls and seeped out at night like an eating ooze, locusts stripped the gardens, then the unseasonal migration of horseflies who ate at them.

What the insects didn't finish, the hordes of starving and

desperate people took care of. After they swarmed over the house like the insects, not much remained. Pierce stood in the debris like Scarlett O'Hara, his hands in fists, and vowed never again.

Pierce had needed a place to hide and hold his stuff. He moved what was left of his home into his office building downtown and hired his first security team to protect it.

Parker's worthless ex-husband had gone M.I.A., and a fine thing that was, leaving him the boy who now had little more to recommend him than a quick mind, a stunning ambition, and an impressive juvenile record.

Pierce hadn't known what he and his grandson would do, how they would live, until Frank Harvey came to him. Money couldn't make water from nothing or food grow from dust, but Frank had kept his eyes low as he very nearly begged to save them all. Frank's project plans and blueprints had been innovative and realistic. Pierce had long known that whoever ruled a water source ruled every one dependent on that water. His dad had taught him that.

Now it was all ruined because of an aging conspiracy theorist and a petulant little boy with daddy issues. He had ruled his kingdom with a fair and just hand. They'd had peace and relative prosperity for almost a decade. They all should have been thankful and been satisfied. At the least, they could have left it alone. But no. They couldn't manage to do that.

Anne leaned down and pulled the cloth from Pierce's mouth.

"How did you know I was here?" Pierce asked.

"Frank asked me to set you free," Anne said. "Soldiers are coming. Frank believes you have information and weapons that might help. I'm not so sure."

"What happened?"

Anne went into the kitchen and poured a glass of water. She held a sip to his lips.

"If you're going to talk, I'm putting on the gag and I won't release your hands," Anne said. She waited for a moment to ensure Pierce's silence and then untied his hands.

"Come join us," Anne said.

Pierce rubbed his wrists as he watched her exit the room.

Pierce's Nomad signaled and the image of a blood-soaked Zach Garland appeared in his living room. Pierce felt the sting of his loss as he looked at his young grandson.

"Zach."

"Sir," Zach said.

"You look like hell," Pierce said.

"There was a little trouble with Shreveport."

"I saw." Pierce pointed toward the screen up on his wall."

"You watched?" Zach asked.

"I reviewed the footage."

Pierce assumed that Zach was disappointed because he couldn't use the lies he had prepared.

"I want to come in," Zach said.

Pierce had had an affair with his maid during the isolation for Covid-19 and she got pregnant. His girlfriend at the time had been none too happy. Shortly after being found out, both women moved out. Pierce had never had an opportunity to meet his daughter. He didn't know he had a grandson until Zach was fifteen years old.

Zach was a naughty and troublesome grandson. It had become almost immediately evident that he couldn't have Zach inside the dome. Zach schemed and manipulated people. Pierce knew that Zach had run frequent scams. At that time, all Pierce could think to do was move Zach outside to be looked after by an ex-marine friend of his. That was his version of extended time-out.

It broke his heart to send Anne out too. She was also like family to Pierce. He sent Anne to the police outside and asked Zach to keep an eye on her, but really he wanted Anne close to Zach so she would watch over him, keep him in line.

"Zach, I know you've been stealing from me. I know about your black market. I've known for a while." Pierce was exhausted and angry. He had to punish Zach, seriously punish him.

To his surprise, Zach didn't try denying it. "I'm sorry," he said. "I'll do better. I promise." That was a first for Zach.

"Zach. It's too late. Apologies aren't going to be enough now." Pierce turned away and disconnected the call. He left Zach outside the gate to do his worst. He was a survivor. He'd be fine.

Pierce grabbed a bottle off his bar and downed a quarter of it in one long swig. He stared at the image that filled the room from his Nomad. He waited for his eyes to focus.

Now they'll come with guns. Long ago, the government under

the first martial law took his own weapons. He had not been able to reacquire an arsenal since Shreveport set a perimeter around them, claiming to protect them from outside marauders who would take what they have, but also preventing them from arming themselves or from making other alliances.

Since then, he'd put together an armory of sorts holding anything he could purchase that could potentially be a weapon. But, it wasn't much. A craftsman carefully made bows, arrows and spears at a snail's pace. Pierce had stored knives, batons and stun guns, those still allowed for police and security forces. But Shreveport had assault rifles and police-issue 35-caliber handguns. Shreveport's police had never traded in their armaments. They shot and killed anyone who had tried to take them.

Pierce heard that, several miles beyond the perimeter of the lake, a tent city had sprung up. Waiting. Soon everyone would know they were vulnerable.

Waco. Oh God. Waco. Waco had tanks. If they were going to war, he needed a commanding officer. He had two seconds-in-command, Vice Presidents. One had disappeared. Broadnack had probably holed up somewhere, nowhere close to the open hostility. Broadnack was a coward. The other had just defied him, tied him up and left him on his bedroom floor. Frank had humiliated him. But, Frank was still the smartest person on Pierce's staff, the person Pierce most truly trusted.

Pierce shakily set up his Nomad to point at himself. "Message to all," he said. "Hell," he said not meaning for it to be heard, but it bounced back to him from his own screen and the Jumbotron at the gate. He straightened up, smoothed his clothes and started his address.

"Ten years ago, when we first realized this masterful idea for saving the food chain," his hand limply formed an arc that represented everything around him, "I made a deal with our friends in Shreveport." He paused, looking at his half-full bottle, but decided drinking it would not inspire confidence. "We bartered. We traded their abundant rainwater for our abundant sunlight in order to make our dream of food grow. And it worked. We created the thing that everyone wanted. We have maintained a shaky peace treaty with Shreveport where they provide water and preserve our safety via a heavily-armed patrol outside our perimeter in return for a reasonable portion of our food supply."

What the hell, he thought. He grabbed the bottle, turned his back and grabbed a quick gulp. He watched himself take the drink on the Jumbotron outside his window.

"Now, ah, that treaty is broken. They're coming. Grab weapons, food and fresh water, anything useful you have and get inside the dome. It's your best chance."

He signed off.

Zach was gone. Anne was no longer his girl. Frank rejected him. Even Charlie was MIA. He was alone and going to war.

Chapter 47

Frank had gotten his son back into his life. His son, his son's girlfriend, his son's friend, his son's friend's girlfriend, a wheezy old man who was fine after a few hours on fresh air and a cop were all now living in his five-hundred-square-foot houseboat. As a precaution, he had moved Alex and Anne from the outside in. Alex invited Ved, Sonia, Jared and Trix. All the kids slept in the bedroom and Ved took the sofa. That left the floor for Anne and Frank. Anne went and got a couple of mats from the training center in the Wagner Building. They smelled like sweat.

To keep an eye on them, Wagner had posted two security guards who wouldn't stay outside where Frank wanted them and further crowded his space. It had been less than twenty hours since Frank and Alex came off the surface of the dome and Frank already longed for the good old days when he lived alone.

At least Alex had fixed his accounts so that Frank could feed all these people, at least for now.

"How long will it take for Waco to get here?" Frank asked.

"Any time now," Anne said.

Alex sat cross-legged on the floor with a computer on his lap running searches on an antique database stored on an external hard drive. He looked for topics like ancient weapons. "We need an inventory of what resources are available," Alex said.

"Like Pierce would give us that," Anne scoffed.

"He would if we have some good ideas, well maybe not good ideas, but ideas," Alex said.

Ved polished off Frank's last canister of fresh air. "You have something in mind?"

"You know the term 'running the gauntlet?' The main entrance to the dome is our most vulnerable access point. We could rig the entrance with deterrents, sharpened sticks or the like, something too small to run through without getting hurt."

"That sounds desperate," Jared said.

"Don't we need all the sharp things in our hands?" Trix asked, but nobody had an answer. Trix sat in a corner, shaking. Jared sat next to her, patting her hand.

"I'll take that position with my officers," Anne said.

Alex nodded at this.

Anne had eight officers who were not hurt. Wagner had a security force of twenty. Twenty-eight against an army. It was clear to Frank that everyone would have to fight and they still didn't have a chance.

"What about the hole at the top of the dome?" Alex asked.

"There's a hole?" Jared asked.

"Yes. In the power station. There is a long narrow hallway, like in a submarine, too crowded to station men. In the submarine hallway, there is a shaft that leads up to a vent at the top of the dome," Alex said.

Frank nodded. He had wondered how Alex had gotten to the top of the dome the day before. "Is it easy to climb?"

"Not for you," Alex answered.

"We should use the hole," Ved said. "I saw a movie once that had Greek Fire in it. Greek Fire is a concoction that keeps fire burning even when you attempt to put it out with water. Does that database tell how to make it?

"No," Alex said. "There's not as much as I hoped about how to make weapons, but I'm still looking. I think the database has been cleansed. I did find a bit about making dynamite."

"That'll get the job done," Ved said.

Alex was disturbed. "Am I the only one who thinks there's something wrong about this approach?"

"No, we all think that something's wrong," Frank said.

Sonia filled in the blanks speaking for Alex. "What he's saying is, we should be looking for ways to make peace, not ways to make war."

That was such an Etta thing to say. Frank liked this quiet girl who reminded him so much of his wife. It was about finding the best in a bad situation, like the cactus that survived in the most inhospitable climate.

"Etta would have found a peaceful solution," Frank agreed. "Etta could focus her thoughts and intents on what was true. She believed people do what they do for a reason. If she could figure out their truth, she believed all people were mostly good at their core." Frank wondered what Alex believed. Did his son trust people, as Etta had, or guard against them, as his father did?

Sonia leaned to him and said, "When things seem worst, men usually find a way to put themselves in harm's way." Frank wondered why Sonia did not include him among men.

Anne, the warrior, took Sonia's hand. "It will be only hours, maybe minutes, before we must defend our lives. We have no choice."

"There's always a choice," Sonia said.

They were all surprised by a knock at the door and surprised further when Pierce Wagner let himself in. Like a big bully, he shoed Frank out of the desk chair and occupied it. Frank let him. Wagner turned his attention to the wheezy old man.

"Kolli," Wagner said.

"Pierce."

"Wait," interjected Frank. "You two know each other."

"Of course, I worked for his think tank before the pandemic started," Ved said, "until he and his cabal monetized people's despair."

"How'd you expect me to pay for all these improvements? Vaccines. The biodome, pipeline and reservoir. Food. I chose us over everyone else," Wagner said.

"Some of us," Ved said. "I can think of twenty-two scientists who would disagree?"

"You can't blame me for that," Wanger protested. "You moved out."

"You kicked us out," Ved countered.

"You could have stayed. You knew my terms. Instead, you chose to be high-minded.

"Yeah. You're faultless," Alex said.

Wagner wiped around. "You've made quite the mess, Mr. Sarcastic." Wagner pointed at Alex. "Are you proud of yourself?"

"Me?" Alex looked genuinely surprised.

"And you." Wagner pointed at Anne. "I trusted you."

"Alex isn't your problem." Anne said. "There's security footage of him at exactly the moment the system crashed. He's not at fault and neither am I."

"Annie. Why are you so mad at me? What did I do?" Wagner asked. "All I ever wanted was to make things better. I spent a fortune...."

"So, what's to the left?" Anne interrupted.

"Food. Like I said." Wagner brought the level of his voice down. If not, in a minute he would have been shrieking. Calmly he clarified, "Have you ever noticed the cans?"

"Cans of what?"

"Everything. Canned goods last, so Shreveport sends out foraging parties to ghost towns to retrieve all they can find to trade with us and the..."

"...and the rest of the affluent," Ved interjected, "who somehow still managed to have hard times slide off their backs like water off a duck."

"The station in the arid to the left is Shreveport's," Wagner said. "We trade an additional amount of our fresh food for canned goods and other kinds of supplies we can't materialize out of thin air. We had a treaty, a really good treaty. It was working or hadn't you noticed? At least it was – until you raided Shreveport's payment."

Anne stared mouth agape. "It wasn't working. You traded the lives of the many so a few people could live well."

"And just what was the alternative? All of us die? Wagner asked."

"Those that have, give a little. Those that need, get a little," Anne said.

"You got anything to drink?" Wagner asked. They all looked incredulous.

"Water," Frank said, yet no one moved to get him a glass.

Wagner responded to their faces. "This room has some of the best minds we have left," he said. "Did you know that Kolli was a Rhodes scholar, went to Oxford? That's where we met."

All eyes turned toward Ved's astonished and wary expression. "Did you know that Pierce dropped out of grad school to master in self-service?"

"We're all in trouble. Fortunately my interests and your interests align," Pierce shot back. Great pounding booms started from outside the dome. "They always have."

Anne stood and looked out the window. The Shreveport soldiers were shooting their rifles at the locking mechanism of the gateway of the dome, however, the locks were inside under the glass. The bullets hit without nicking the surface. She went out on the swimming deck and ordered one of her officers to go to the gate and check for spider veins. How long could the infrastructure withstand a pounding like this?

"Have you heard of metallic glass?" Wagner asked. "It's strong like steel and flexible like rubber while being clear like glass. I made the surface double thick for just this day. Now I bet you're glad you didn't bring down our security system?"

"I could have brought it back up any time," Alex replied.

"You've been planning for this?" Frank's mouth was agape.

"No. I've been preparing. It's not the same. I'm hoping you're the ones with the plan."

Alex hesitated, thought it through and finally he spoke. "We're going to focus on the gateway. We think that's our most vulnerable point."

"Vulnerability. Good start," Wagner said.

"Actually, the dome's most vulnerable at the top where the glass is thinnest," Frank said.

"I can't believe they would risk the dome," Anne said. "They're bound to be looking for another way inside."

Oh my God!" Wagner jumped up. "My grandson, Zach. I didn't let him come in and take shelter in the dome."

"The loading dock." Frank caught on. "One of the bays was open."

"And Zach Garland knows where it is," Anne added.

Wagner pulled up his Nomad. "Where is Zach?"

"Zach Garland not found."

"How can that be?"

"It means he is out of range." Ved explained.

"Where did you leave him?" Alex asked.

On a camel. Going into the wasteland.

"I have a few guns," Wagner led the way. "And other weapons."

Chapter 48

From Wagner's tiny office, Frank opened the bookcase entrance that revealed Wagner's hidden living room. Anne waved her officers inside. They shuffled and crowded into the living room. Their faces were a mixture of awe and anger. Frank and Alex brought up the rear and closed the bookcase entrance. They had six real guns, twenty stun guns and twelve hunting knives among them.

Ved and Wagner sat on the sofa in the living room. Wagner called them the second line. He had no intention of moving. Wagner had found Ved another couple of canisters of fresh air. Wagner held his decanter of Parker's whiskey close to his chest, but at least he wasn't drinking. They looked chummy.

"You've forgiven him," Alex said incredulously to Ved.

"Let's just say we've come to an arrangement," Ved countered. "I've agreed to keep security features, but to modify the Nomad's embedded chip to allow people access to the dome."

"Approved people," Wagner corrected.

"All people," Ved shot back. "Anybody can come into the dome, use the resources, barter at the store."

"All locals," Wagner clarified. "All people who live in Austin. Otherwise, what's the purpose of the chip then?"

"Keep people from getting greedy – especially you," Frank said.

Alex wasn't sure what to think and so he put a finger to his lips to quiet them.

"Screen One," Wagner whispered into his Nomad. "Show interior garage security cam." There were two Shreveport officers exploring the bay. The south-side wall was covered in industrial piping that went from the concrete floor up to iron beams that ran the length of the ceiling. Heavy pipes held up shelves of storage bins. One of the soldiers set down his rifle on the floor and lifted himself up by the strength of his arms to the second shelf. He opened a bin. He handed down a second bin the other soldier.

"What's out there?" Anne asked meaning the bins.

"Nothing important," Wagner replied.

"Screen Two. Garage exterior cam." Two additional soldiers stood on the loading dock, watching the approach of the Shreveport army. They were coming but weren't quite here yet. Lots of them. Too many.

Alex stared at the image for a long time. It was like he was trying to decipher a puzzle.

"How do you close the bay doors?" Alex asked Wagner.

Wagner pointed to a red button near the open entrance on the opposite side of the room.

"You can't close the bay from your Nomad?"

"It's a safety feature," Wagner responded snidely, "in case someone turns off the power."

"Are they strong? The doors?"

"Double-width hurricane doors. Extra strong locks." He pointed to a slide bar that could be shoved across the length of the bay doors.

Alex took Anne's arm. "I want to say one thing before we go in there. You're angry about Officer June." He looked into the barely controlled hostility in the room. "Many of you are. If you act on it, if you kill even one of them, this will never end. They kill us. We kill them. It could go on for years. Disarm them. Shoot them in the leg or the shoulder if you must shoot, but don't kill them. Agreed?"

They shuffled.

Alex purposefully charged down the hall. Anne followed with the others. Frank closed the bookcase door behind them.

Alex silently opened the garage door and slipped in without the two soldiers, who were shifting through an open bin, noticing him. Their rifles lay on the ground, temporarily forgotten. Their heads shot up as Anne and her troops stormed in. Alex kicked the soldiers' rifles toward Anne, and then scrambled up the piping and shimmied across a steel beam toward the open bay door.

Frank picked up the rifles and took a stand at the door. Anne watched as her officers roughed up and arrested the two greedy Shreveport soldiers and then she followed Alex deeper into the dimly lit garage.

The first soldier from outside rushed in, firing toward Alex, but the soldier was blinded by a severe change in light as Frank flipped the switch and flooded the space. Anne was there to knock away his rifle with a roundhouse kick. Once he was down, she delivered a couple savage blows to his face.

Alex jumped down in front of the open bay door. He hit the red button. The fourth soldier slipped under the falling door. He raised his rifle toward Alex. Frank sprayed bullets over his head.

"Back off of my son," Frank said.

Alex listened for the locks engaging and then he slid the heavy bar across the closed bay doors.

Chapter 49

Frank sat on Wagner's deck and watched the sun set outside. It was an eerie effect to watch Molotov cocktails break overhead on the intact surface of the dome. Fire fell to the ground outside causing more trouble for the Shreveport Army than for them. *What was the purpose?* Frank wondered. Fire wouldn't breach the dome. Probably to intimidate, to scare them.

It was not surprising that the Shreveport Army had been quiet through the heat of the day with the first attack starting as night fell. During the day, the Shreveport Army hadn't been able to break through the steel barrier of the bay doors. They also tried shooting out the glass at the dome's gateway, but the small caliber bullets in their assault rifles didn't have the range to have enough impact. So, they had grown quiet. Waiting.

Frank had built Alex's gauntlet at both the gateway and in the secret hallway in Wagner's lair—strange-looking structures of spikes made out of rebar beanpoles from Frank's garden. It would prevent easy entry. Anne's forces were positioned at these two lethal-looking structures. Waiting.

In the power station, Frank and Alex had built platforms to allow easy access to the opening of the dome. Frank rigged up an irrigation system that flowed a thin film of water over the outside surface of the dome. This helped to keep it cool and less likely to crack against the firestorm. It was also slick, making attempts to climb the dome from the outside more difficult.

And, it was pretty. The thickness of the dome made the flowing water appear soft, like being inside of a gentle waterfall. The firebombs made rainbows of color as they burst and fizzled.

Frank grabbed a couple of wineglasses from Wagner's bar and a bottle of white before he walked down to the gate to see Anne.

"Detective, would you like to join me?" He held up the bottle for her to inspect.

Anne protested as he dragged her along. "I can't leave my post."

"You need a rest. It has been a crazy day with a long night

ahead. Have a little glass of wine. This stress, anticipation, is exhausting. Rebuild your strength."

She protested his arguments, but finally, Anne sat down with Frank at the end of the pier. She relaxed a bit. She watched the light display going on over her head.

"I love the night. It's the only time of day when it's cool and quiet. Pierce did me such a favor when he kicked me out of the dome. I'd walk for hours."

"It's dangerous to walk around alone at night." Frank was surprised at the bravado of this woman.

"Too bad it won't last," she said.

"What? The fire storm?"

"No. The dome."

"The alloy combined with the structure of steel and wire...."

"That's amazing. Really whose idea was that? Not Pierce. He buys. He doesn't think."

"Assistant. Man I work with ... I think. He knew about it."

"What's his name?"

"I'm not very good with names." Frank hemmed for a minute. "Pony."

"Pony? What's his real name. You don't know," Anne said. "How long have you worked with him?"

Frank's face was blank.

"What's my name?" Anne asked.

Frank looked shy with a crooked grin. He didn't immediately answer.

"You don't know my name, do you?"

"Detective," Frank teased.

"No. My name is not Detective."

He smiled. "Anne. Detective Anne Roget."

Anne went back to looking at the sky. Frank put his arm around Anne. It was nice, until...

Alex ambled by and gestured to his dad. "He's not such a good bet."

To Frank's surprise, Anne answered, "Yes, he is."

Chapter 50

What was it called when you can see by the light of a full moon? Anne couldn't remember. Maybe a farmer's term. Harvest moon? And the effect of the full moon – that she remembered, that was called lunacy.

Anne and Frank soon followed Alex toward the Wagner building with Frank splitting off from her at the secret hallway behind the bookcase.

Anne sat down next to Sonia at a long table in Pierce's secret dining room just off Pierce's secret living room. Pierce had insisted that she cover his family's walnut table with a rubber pad. It was important to him that his secret things be protected.

Sonia was surrounded by an assortment of red, green and gold glass Christmas ornaments. She filled each ball with ground charcoal, sulfur and a fertilizer that was primarily a nitrate. She was making gunpowder, which was not available itself, but each component could be found. Pierce knew this and had stored up.

Anne picked up a filled ornament. It was red with a faceted surface that made to look like a cut diamond. On it, was a hand painted scene. These were not the Christmas ornaments that you get at the store twelve in a box. She added a wick and sealed the little bomb with malleable wax.

Ved had gotten the idea for using Christmas ornaments from a movie. "I think it was one of the Iron Man movies," he said "or maybe Home Alone." Ved watched a lot of old movies.

They planned to launch the ornaments from a tee shirt air cannon that Pierce had in a different closet from where he kept his family's Christmas decorations. They didn't know if the glass balls would hold up to the launch or not, but, if they did, the flaming explosive bulbs were sure to break on impact.

Alex entered the room. He sat on the sofa in the living room and picked up his drawing pad. He held it in front of him.

Sonia looked back and forth between Anne and Alex. She was sensitive to the tension between the two and left the room.

"Why are you still so angry with your father?" Anne asked Alex. He jumped up and disappeared around a corner to rummage around in one of the closets. "You know he tried to provide you and your mother with food."

Alex dropped his drawing pad on the table surface, opened it and sat down. He was designing a scaffold to hold the air canon, what was essentially still just a peashooter, steady and in place at the rim of the air vent at the top of the dome.

"What's the range on the canon?" he asked.

"Up to about three-hundred feet. You should assume the distance wouldn't be so great. And you didn't answer the question."

"Three-hundred feet. What's the point? This'll never work."

"Why are you so angry?"

Alex was quiet for a minute. "He left my mother right when she needed him most. That's what I can't forgive."

"You should talk to him. There are things you don't know."

"He abandoned us. What more is there to know?"

"Well," she said. "In my investigation, I did a fair amount of research into your family. For one thing, she was the one who filed for divorce. She left him. He didn't leave her. I don't think he wanted the divorce."

It was clear that Alex hadn't known that. "She must have had her reasons." He continued to cling to his resentments.

"Frank's not a villain. He's a fallible man who hasn't made as many mistakes as you think." Anne stared him down. "Talk to him."

Alex held up his sketch for her to admire.

"Ask him about the baby," she said.

Alex looked interested. "Tell me about the baby."

"I don't know. I only suspect. You have to ask your father."

Sonia rejoined Anne in the dining room. Sonia picked up a gold ball with a wreath on it and sighed.

Chapter 51

Alex kissed Sonia on the cheek, and then relocated to the submarine hallway in the power station. He and Frank had spent most of the day building a series of connected platforms that allowed access to the roof vent from inside the building. Alex climbed to the top-most point and hunched on the scaffold's tallest platform. He rested his modified air canon out the vent on the top surface of the dome. The metallic glass was shiny from the thin film of water Frank piped over the dome's surface to keep it slick and cool.

Frank sat on a platform one level below Alex and handed him hard, rubber stress balls. Alex shot a stress ball at maximum velocity at an invader who had climbed the dome's outer surface, sledgehammer in hand. At the distance the climber was from the top, being hit with the ball just annoyed him.

"Hmm."

Outside, the scene was surreal. Soldiers in uniforms that looked like Desert Storm, with rifles or pistols, flanked two sections of the dome near the train station. They had changed their tactics a bit. This time when the captain yelled, "Ready, Set, Fire," all the soldiers aimed at the same two-foot square area about three sections up toward the top of the dome where the glass was weakest. They sent three forays of shots that the insiders couldn't see coming in the dark and then a man with a sledgehammer climbed up the dome to see if the metallic glass had cracked. He'd give any cracks a couple of good whacks hoping they would give way. Alex wondered what that dumbass thought would happen to him if the dome shattered and he was standing sixty feet above ground covered with broken glass. Silly. They were fighting rifles with an air canon and rubber balls. And winning, he thought, at least for today. The invading soldiers were being worn down by heat and hunger.

"They're all focusing on the same panel of glass," Alex said.

"Yes." Frank said.

"I guess they figure they can repair one grid panel."

"Or even two."

Alex estimated that there were maybe two hundred marauders. They had arrived quickly, likely from camps not as far away as Shreveport. The main army was still to come. They lived in tents set up out in the open. Other than the train station, there was no place close enough to the dome to protect themselves from the blaring heat during the day and the snakes at night.

He recognized them. They were desperate, just like the outsiders who lived five hundred feet from where the invaders were camped. For all he knew, many of them might be the zombies from Austin who couldn't or wouldn't come inside when Wagner called. They were all the same people and soon he might have to make the choice to kill some of them.

"Let me try," Frank said. Frank popped three balls in quick succession at the shoulder of the man with the sledgehammer. The soldier spun, lost his footing and slipped a little. Frank hooted. Alex passed up refills as fast as Frank could shoot them. Frank cheered at his success when the soldier finally fell on his butt, his sledgehammer sliding a few feet away from him. Alex looked incredulous. "What?" Frank said. "I was a gamer."

"It'll be different with fire balls."

Frank nodded.

Alex understood the need to push them back, but the Shreveport soldiers hadn't figured out the mosh pit idea that Austin outsiders used to break his and his father's fall. When he and his Dad had fallen, crowds of people rushed together to catch them, break their fall. When Sledgehammer tumbled down, he would fall all the way to hard surfaces: cement and rocks. Stupid. Alex wanted to yell out advice.

He and Frank took turns shooting the air canon until the raider retreated. Frank took a break, squatting on the lower platform. Frank's face was bathed in the light of a full moon framed by the opening at the top of the dome.

Frank held up a small box that contained about a dozen stress balls. "Is this the last of them?"

Alex was lost in thought. He stared at this man, his father, who he barely knew. "Tell me about the baby," Alex said.

"What?" Frank looked confused.

"Julietta."

Realization hit. "I called her Grace, for her mother. It means generosity of spirit."

"Mom named her Julie. I added the ending."

"Julietta," Frank tried out the name. "I like it."

Alex analyzed the fleeting look on Frank's face. It wasn't shame or guilt as Alex thought it should be. It was something more like pride. Could that be? Alex watched as Frank shut down.

"These are personal matters," Frank said. "I won't discuss them with you."

"Yes, they're very personal to me," Alex replied.

Frank wouldn't meet his eyes. Still, his look was odd.

"Oh my God!" Alex said. "You're protecting me from the truth." He recognized the expression. He had seen it in the mirror. "What did you do that was so horrible?" He stopped.

Frank turned himself into a statue, flexed all his muscles to hold the emotions. His jaw locked and veins popped on his neck. Despite his best effort, tears blurred his eyes.

"It wasn't you," Alex felt the blood drain from his face, but couldn't stop now. "It was her. What did she do?"

"You have such an idealized view of your mother," Frank paused, treading lightly on Alex's soul. "She was the most authentic person I ever knew. She was caring, giving and loving. That was the real her, but she wasn't perfect."

Alex set his mind to making sense of what he knew, figuring it out.

"Your Sonia reminds me a lot of your mother. Sonia seems very gentle and loving too."

Something about the baby, Alex thought. Something that led to the divorce. His mouth gapped. "She had an affair."

Frank's look of surprise was all the confirmation he needed. "I guess you're not a little boy any longer, are you?"

Alex climbed up to the top platform and took a breath at the opening. The dome was getting too close for him. "With who?" he asked. When Frank didn't immediately answer, Alex asked, "Was it Charlie?"

"I don't know what Charlie and Etta's relationship became, but it wasn't sexual. Not back then. "

Frank was aloof, shutting down again. Alex could see him become more detached. If he didn't get an answer this instant, he might never get one. "Say something."

There was a radiologist, at the hospital I think." He paused to think. "Love can be brutal," Frank tentatively began, "but I would have eventually forgiven her the affair. She lied, cheated and contracted sickness that brought death for our baby, but I would have forgiven her. She still fills my dreams. She's all I want." He paused. "Except you."

It was a hard admission and Alex wanted to give him a little something – a truth for a truth. "The last words on my lips to my mother were a lie."

Frank was interested. He looked toward his son.

"I told her I was going to school, but I wasn't," Alex filled in.

Frank's lips turned up a bit at one corner. "I'm sure she would rather have believed you were going to school than know you lied to her."

"She found me out. My teacher called. That was the last thing she knew about me, that I lied to her," Alex replied. "So, if you wanted her so much, how did you end up divorced?"

"She couldn't forgive herself."

Alex didn't need Frank to explain how she got sick. Medicines had been in short supply for years. Alex had seen untreated illness and hunger waste away his mother, eating at her right down to her muscles and bones.

"Alex," Sonia called from the base of the scaffold. Her voice sounding worried. He slithered down two stories on a support pipe. She handed him a box of Christmas ornaments.

Alex looked at the gaily-colored balls filled with gunpowder. "I know," he said. "I don't like this idea either."

He handed up to Frank a red man-made canon ball with a painted silver bell. To his surprise, Frank set it aside. "Only if we absolutely must," he agreed. Frank stored the box in a corner.

"Gonorrhea," Alex said as he climbed up next to Frank. "Mom never gave it a name, but I figured it out from the symptoms. I always assumed you gave it to her and then abandoned her."

"No," Frank replied, pain all over his face. "We were all treated with antibiotics. I never contracted it. The strain your mother and the baby had was very resistant to treatment. I think that, at some point, she deemed herself less important than her patients for the very limited supply of meds."

"After the divorce. Then it's my fault."

"Of course not. You were eight years old when we divorced. Don't take that on. She was an adult, a doctor. She made her own choices." Frank looked intent. "Alex, I want you to know I'm sorry for...."

Alex heard the cracking just a few seconds before the one section of the dome shattered. He fell from the platform in a shower of dense glass. The ribbing of the dome collapsed and pushed down the scaffold and everything else in its wake.

The last thing he heard was Sonia's little cry of surprise.

Chapter 52

When he came to, Alex saw his father pull piping off of Sonia. She must have lingered under the platform listening to Alex and Frank talk. Frank checked her for injury.

"Is she okay?" Alex asked anxiously.

"Concussion, maybe. She's out. And I think her arm is broken. You?" Frank asked.

Alex did a quick appraisal and found himself mostly intact. He stood. "I'm okay."

Frank scooped Sonia into his arms. "Let's get her to triage." Frank walked with a limp.

"You're hurt too. I'll carry her," Alex said as he pulled her from Frank's arms.

Sledgehammer appeared at the hole. He hadn't fallen through as Alex had predicted. The soldier pulled off his shirt to protect his hands from the broken shards of glass. Behind him, others lined up to gingerly pick their way through the hole Sledgehammer had made. The soldiers were about sixty feet from the ground at a hole that was perilous with sharp edges. This seemed the only hole. So entry was possible only in the narrow submarine hallway where they were.

Suddenly Wagner appeared at the ground level entryway with an AK47. He peppered the air with bullets.

Sledgehammer grabbed a red wet spot on his arm.

Anne sneaked up from behind Wagner and disarmed him. She signaled for her officers to hold back. The confined space of the hallway made too many people more of a hindrance than a help.

Anne swung like an aerial ballerina from the vertical bars of the scaffolding, kicking out. It was a dance of aggression, and Sledgehammer went down. Anne shot a fully automatic burst from the AK47 to discourage more of the Shreveport soldiers from descending. They fell back their position a bit. Anne and Alex dragged out Sledgehammer and she posted a few guards to watch the hole. Anne gave one of the officers the AK47.

Alex went down on one knee next to Sonia. She came around slowly. She winced as Alex cradled her to his chest.

"Are you crazy?" he asked Wagner. Sonia's eyes came wide at the frantic tone of his voice. "How many more of those rifles do you have hidden?"

"Just the one," Wagner said. "But I have plenty of clips for it."

"I hate this." Alex said. He didn't want to chance one more person he knew getting hurt or dying. In his mind, he was screaming.

Frank started to climb the scaffolding.

"What are you doing?" Alex asked. "Running away?"

Frank had that hurt look again. "What we should have done in the first place. What Etta would have done. I'm going to go talk to them."

"I didn't mean to say that," Alex said. "Wait. Don't go."

Frank looked torn, torn between doing what he thought was right for his family and doing what Alex wanted him to do.

"We'll come up with a plan we can do together," Alex said.

Chapter 53

During the night, Frank saw Alex change. Frank wanted to be whatever Alex wanted in this conflict, whomever he needed. If Alex thought he was aloof, he would be present. If Alex thought he was selfish, he would be altruistic. If Alex thought he was a coward, he would be a hero. He would take whatever ground he needed to retain the progress he had made with his son.

The Shreveport army had retreated. In a couple hours, the sun would rise and sap the energy right from them all. Frank walked through the tail end of the night toward the Wagner Tower. Three people had been seriously injured defending the hole blown into the dome, two from Shreveport and one from Austin. Minor injuries waited for treatment in a line that went halfway down the pier. It could have been much worse.

Frank entered the Wagner building, a cool haven in a burning world. He took the elevator to the medical center on the second floor. Alex lay alongside of Sonia, on the bed, touching down the length of her. He slipped a ring onto Sonia's finger. "I love you too," Alex whispered into her ear. Sonia's eyelids fluttered and fell heavy. He curled into Sonia's armpit as she fell asleep.

Frank sat down into an empty chair beside the bed. Alex's eyes blinked a few times and then focused on Frank.

"I'm sorry, Alex" Frank said.

"For what?"

It was a quiet query. Was Alex looking for a list of Frank's faults? For what was he apologizing? I wish I had been a better father to you, he thought. I wish I had known what was going on. He examined Alex; thought about what Alex wanted and said, "I'm sorry I moved into the dome. I wanted to be a hero. I truly believed that everyone would die if not for my farm."

"I understand you had your reasons for doing the things you did."

He was quoting Etta. Was that an acceptance of his apology? Frank thought it was.

Anne appeared at the door. She touched Sonia's forehead and kissed her cheek as Sonia slept.

"Start Routine," Alex said.

Alex held up his Nomad and took some footage of Anne holding Sonia's hand. Anne smiled. It was a beautiful image, touching. The film of Anne and Sonia appeared on the Jumbotron.

"I created a program to scan the live camera footage, both inside and out, to recognize happy, smiling faces."

Two Shreveport soldiers laughed together, the arm of one lay heavily on the shoulder of the other. "Each time someone smiles, a camera captures it and displays it there." He pointed at the big screen. Alex smiled. He couldn't help himself. In a few seconds, his smile was ten-foot tall. It went on like that, the images growing faster and closer together as people enjoyed it. "It's to remind us we're all one."

Pierce sat on his deck, watching the smiling faces on the Jumbotron. Tears slipped unbidden and unrestrained down his cheeks. On the street below him, faces turned up to the images and smiled in their turn. In a few seconds, those faces appeared in the sky.

Mixed in, Pierce had seen Zach shaking hands with the Shreveport Commander, a sleazy grin on his face.

"Goodbye," Pierce said. "He's your problem now."

Chapter 54

The day was hot. Scorching hot. Intense rays from the sun glared in a way that indicated it could only be another 112-degree day.

His men were tired, hungry and burnt by the sun. The Shreveport command had as many men down to dehydration as to the battle. If they didn't win soon, the Commander didn't know how much longer he could order them to go on and they would still be able to comply. He was beginning to wonder himself at how much of a win this relentless place would be.

The Commander heard an odd chirping noise. It wouldn't give up, also relentless. He looked around on his desk and under his bed, but could not see from where it came.

"Commander," the face of one of his soldiers appeared at his tent flap.

"Yes."

"Look." The soldier pointed to the large, flashing sign over the gate of the dome where the happy faces were displayed. It scrolled, "Commander, I've left you a phone in your locker." A phone? He hadn't seen a working phone in fifteen years.

The Commander went to a footlocker where he kept his clothes and other personal belongings. The soldier at his entrance looked as anxious as he felt. Others were beginning to gather outside.

The Commander lifted the top. The chirping sound grew louder. Did they have magic? How did they get this object into his locker with no one seeing or hearing a thing?

"Maybe you shouldn't touch it?" the soldier said.

He agreed, but what choice did he have? He couldn't appear weak in front of his men.

"Back up," he warned his man.

The Commander picked it up. Good start, it didn't blow off his hand. He answered and an image appeared on the Jumbotron. It was a boy with a shaved head and intense green eyes. The boy signaled off screen and an old man with shiny silver hair came to flank him looking none to too happy.

"Commander," the boy said.

"Yes," he responded warily.

"Check the messenger bag under your desk."

The Commander could see it. A satchel under his desk. Here it was. The bomb that would end his life.

"I appreciate your apprehension," the boy said, "But it's not a trick."

The Commander lifted one corner of the bag's flap.

"Peaches are in season," a wild-haired man with the same intense green eyes stepped on-screen and gave everyone a wave.

The Commander looked inside the bag at the most beautiful, plump peaches he had ever seen.

"Sonia," the boy whispered to someone he could not see. "Hit that key please."

On the Jumbotron, his face appeared on a split screen so everyone on both sides could view him and the boy simultaneously.

"I'm Alex Harvey," he said. "My father, Frank Harvey, grew those peaches and other fresh food you've been enjoying over the last ten years."

Frank said. "They're nothing but juicy and delicious."

Crap, the Commander thought. He debated with himself. He had to try one, but could they have poisoned it or laced it with a sleeping potion. He reached deep into the bag and tossed a peach to the soldier at his entrance. The soldier didn't seem to care if the peach was poisoned or not. He took a bite. They all waited a few seconds, but nothing happened except the soldier finished off the peach.

"Distribute these." The Commander kept one for himself and handed over the messenger bag.

"This is Pierce Wagner of the Wagner Company." Alex pointed to the old man with the silver hair. "Most of us did not know about your deal with Wagner. When we discovered that he was shipping out food, we assumed it was for selfish purposes."

The Commander recognized Wagner's name. He had a counterpart in Shreveport, a despot named Flynn. Flynn barricaded himself and a few of the richie-rich in Shreveport's best resort and casino. If you wanted a job, if you wanted to eat, you had to pander to Flynn.

"We still have many people here who are starving, as I'm sure you do as well. We regret the disruption to your food supply."

The Commander didn't know what to make of that. They were fighting a war and this boy was apologizing. He couldn't seem to form a coherent response, so he said nothing.

"We have lost many of our people to starvation, to illness and now to warfare. It's stupid and preventable," the wild-haired man said.

"Did he just call us stupid?" his officer said. "Now, hold on..." he started.

"I see that you're a man who, like us, cares for your people. I don't want to fight," Alex said. "I want to barter."

Barter?

"Like I said, my father grows food. Wagner here owns the source code for the Repository," he glanced at the man, "which I'm sure he is happy to share. I, myself, am pretty good with technology. I'm willing to come and set up a network for you in Shreveport. What have you got to lose?"

"No." His father looked at the boy with shock. He hadn't known Alex would make such an offer. "That wasn't part of what we discussed."

The Commander's orders were to get the food supply started again. They didn't say he had to kill everyone to do it. Was this really a chance for a better life for them all?

The father and the boy were arguing in whispered tones. They obstructed his hearing, so he couldn't make out what was being said, but the disagreement added a tone of urgency to the negotiations.

"My first priority is my people, the people I love, the people I live with." The boy returned his attention to the commander. "So is yours. All I'm proposing is that we widen our community. Each gives a little to get a little. Do some good for each other."

The boy was offering a more permanent solution. He looked around at what this town had.

"We want electricity," The commander said. His mouth salivated. They needed electricity. The only place that had power was the generator in the resort. It would make such a huge difference in everyone's daily life. He tried to keep his face neutral to disguise how much it meant to him.

Wagner wagged a finger. "Nah-uh," he said. "You haven't put anything on the table yet."

The Commander hesitated, as if he were considering rejecting the proposition. "We'll go home," The Commander finally said.

The three men waited. Obviously, his offer wasn't high enough.

"And we'll turn on the water supply."

The father looked happy, but it was not good enough for the other two. The boy gently pushed his father off-screen and out of the negotiation.

"And we'll resume our protection of your perimeter."

"Good start," said Alex. "We're back to our original deal. What in exchange for the power?"

The commander thought about it. He wasn't really authorized to make this kind of a deal. He wasn't even sure what they had. Wagner didn't look sure either. He appeared to be weakening. He whispered to the boy maybe telling him he was going too far. "What do you want?" the commander asked.

Alex didn't flinch. "Medicine," he said. "For a power station and a network like ours, I want a continuous source of medical supplies and staff. I hear you have a fully functioning hospital and our last doctor just.... We have no doctors. I'll come help you if you send two doctors with medicine to help us."

"No." The commander heard someone protest off-screen. He thought it might be the kid's father.

Alex didn't take his unwavering eyes off the camera, therefore off him. "I'll come help," he said.

The dad came onscreen. "Then I'll come too. I'm Frank Harvey. I can help you set up a farm. What in exchange for that?"

The boy looked shocked. For the first time, he was speechless. He gathered himself for a minute.

"I'll come with you," the father repeated.

They were already making travel arrangement and the Commander hadn't yet accepted the deal. "I have to talk to my general and the mayor and...."

"This offer lasts ten more seconds," Wagner said. "You must decide. We can tweak the details later, but it's up to you. Peace or War?"

The Commander looked at his men. He saw something in their eyes something he had not seen for a very long time. He saw hope.

"On behalf of the city of Shreveport, I accept."

Chapter 55

In the end, four of them had gone to Shreveport: Frank, Alex, Sonia and Jared. They had stayed six months to get the work started, but they knew that they would be going back and forth for many more years to come.

Anne had stayed behind to wrap up the Black Market case. She had found Charlie dead on the sidewalk below his apartment tower; no doubt it was a suicide. He had apparently been there since before the skirmish with Shreveport.

Shreveport would have been happy to extradite Garland back to Austin, but Pierce said 'no.' He said it was for the best. Frank didn't know what happened to Garland. All he knew was that they didn't have to see him while they were in Shreveport.

When the four returned home, Sonia and Ved moved into the old house with Alex. Alex and Jared removed the split tree and used its lumber and nails from Shreveport to reframe where the roof and walls had failed under its weight. Now, they jumped around like monkeys on the new roof as they installed new solar panels they'd picked up in Shreveport in exchange for a hydroponics garden.

Sonia carried a watering can as she stepped out on the front porch. She watered the prickly-pear cactus in the center of the front yard. Its surface was covered in tiny yellow buds that promised to be beautiful in a week or so.

Frank had built a pergola over the sun garden in the back yard with a built-in watering system that branched from the rebuilt reclamation tower. It was in four quadrants: sunny/wet; sunny/dry; shady/wet and shady/dry. Frank marked what plants would be best suited for what section. Frank tore down a pole that had a battered old plaster owl on it to scare off the birds. Instead, he had erected a four-foot sculpture of a mother and baby. On its base was carved: "In loving memory, Etta Harvey and Julietta Grace Harvey."

Anne joined Frank in the back yard. As she looked at the pergola and the statue, she took Frank's hand. In a minute, Alex and Sonia joined them, arms locked at each other's waist. They stood in silence for a minute, each lost in their own memories.

The sky turned a putrid shade of yellow-green.

Frank nodded at the horizon. In the distance, black clouds hung heavily. At their edge, lightning streaked across the sky. Then boom! Big drops of water hit the ground in front of where they stood.

Alex did a flip and landed on the ground. Jared descended the ladder. "Wow. Is that rain?" he asked.

Frank nodded.

The wind whipped up and then came a deluge. It poured so heavily that it didn't have time to soak into the ground. Instead, it slid off and washed beside the house, down to the street. They followed the flow of water to the front.

Every window and doorway filled with people watching the rainfall. A couple of kids ran into the street to jump into the shoals of the flooding water. Alex grinned and followed them into the rain to play. He was soaked in a second.

Frank and Anne took shelter under the front porch. Frank turned to Anne. "Have you ever seen a storm like this?"

"Once. Just out of the police academy. Twenty one or two."

"Alex was four."

Anne's response was a whisper. "Four," she repeated.

"It will be cooler when it stops. Then, in a day or so, green will perk up in places we didn't know it was hiding."

The gushing water got worse. An orange cone bobbed down the street, riding the current. An odd assortment of trash followed.

"People will be in a good mood, at least for a few days," he continued. "On that night, the night after it stops, would you like to come out to dinner with me?"

"Where would we go?" Anne asked.

"I know a great little farmer's market. Last time I was there, they had a band."

"A band." She nodded her approval.

Alex whooped from the street. His eyes shined with excitement.

"I'd love that," she said.

Alex glowed with child-like innocence. He pulled Frank and Anne with him into the splashing water. Frank came willingly.

Then Frank saw it, recognized it – that look of happiness, of laughter that he had been missing from his son's face for so long and he felt happy too.

Frank splashed Alex with a little water, but he was too wet to really notice.

"Hey Dad," Alex said, halting suddenly. "What if it doesn't stop?"

ABOUT THE AUTHOR

Nancy Smith is a freelance writer of novels, screenplays and short stories. She is also a filmmaker, script analyst, and script supervisor. Nancy is the owner of First Look Script Analysis, operating since December 2005 and First Look Publishing operating since 2016. She lives in Austin, Texas.

Signup for my mailing list at:
http://www.nancysmithwriter.com

Write a comment on Amazon:
http://www.amazon.com

Other Works by Nancy Smith

Books in this Series

This trilogy takes place in the near future. The series describes the world we live in crumbling to ruin through 2045. It's about people living with love and hope at the end of the world.

Book One: *The Universal Vaccine*
(Originally released 2017, New Edition to address Covid-19 released 2022)

A University of Texas at Austin art student comes home to find police on her doorstep. They tell her that her microbiologist mother and engineer father as well as all of her parents' coworkers are dead. Isa wants to understand what happened. She enlists the assistance of an investigative journalist to find out. The pair have no idea where this search will take them.

Book Two: *The Firebrand River*
Released 2022

Every weekend, there's a volleyball party by the Firebrand River until the weekend that strange, green pollution and a mysterious human finger bone shuts down the fun. The owner of the land works with police and an EPA investigator to help solve both an old mystery and a new one.

Book Three: *The Slow Kill*
(Originally released 2014, New Edition to address Covid-19 released 2022)

In the aftermath of a world ravaged by disease, fire, famine and drought, a botanist erects a biodome over Austin's Lake Travis in order to deter evaporation and protect his hydroponics farm. However plans to electrify and seal the dome's exterior, separate the haves from the have nots and force a desperate father apart from his wife and six year old son.

Other books/ebooks by Nancy Smith

Tainted Harvest

This book focuses on the experiences of Tituba, a slave sold in Barbados to Samuel Parris who would eventually become minister in Salem, MA. The book covers her life from the time of her enslavement through the 1692 witch trials. Tituba was the first person to confess to witchcraft. She told a tale at her hearing unlike anything that the Puritans had heard before, a story drawn from her own experiences and spiritual beliefs.

This novel is primarily based on the concepts presented by two noted academics. Linna Caporael went to the top of her class in 1976 when she made the connection between ergot poisoning on the rye during the 1692 growing season in Salam Village and the witch trials. Elaine Breslaw's 1996 book postulated that a clash of cultures between South American native, Tituba, and the New England Puritans added fuel to the fire.

Novellas:

Never Past (Mystery)

Kat Richardson was an ordinary woman, just like you, your mother or your grandmother, until someone chose to make her a victim. Who murdered this sixty-five-year-old retired teacher as she slept alone in her bed — despite the fact that she was secured behind a hard-core bedroom door with a heavy deadbolt. Detective Hedy Werth and her partner, Merton Manes, search for answers.

Picture Postcards (Romantic Drama Novella)

How can Virginia Mae Beauvoir learn to love when the people she most cares about in her life keep abandoning her? What she needs is a good teacher.

Stories Across Time (Short Story Collection)

This collection touches on the human moments of a variety people. The stories are placed in time anywhere within the last ten decades. It's up to the reader to intuit when that might be or if it even matters.

Available at Amazon.com

www.ingramcontent.com/pod-product-compliance
Lightning Source LLC
Chambersburg PA
CBHW061156170626
46809CB00003B/1117